"WONDERFULLY OUTLANDISH."
—*Entertainment Weekly*

"[A] smart and quirky novel . . . How can a story that's loaded with graveyard imagery, involves the death of a child and revolves around the imminent demise of an invalid patriarch and his bedridden wife be so free of gloom and despair? The answer can be found in the way Edgerton lets his deftly etched characters tell the tale from their distinct perspectives in alternating chapters. The narrative efficiently glides forward while the many narrators gracefully reveal their engaging humanity and unique contributions to the world of the living."
—*The Cleveland Plain Dealer*

"IN MEMORY OF JUNIOR is his most elaborate effort yet. Written in a colloquial shorthand that gives a full, flavorful picture of family entanglements, it's a poignant tragicomedy told in 21 voices."
—*The Seattle Times*

"The attitude is edgy Edgerton and the thread is darkly, uproariously comic."
—*The Charlotte Observer*

"Affectionate, affecting . . . Edgerton creates a first-person chorus of distinct Southern voices and uses humor to address the serious matters of family ties in times of change. . . . A fond tribute to the idiosyncrasies and universality of families, IN MEMORY OF JUNIOR is often laugh-aloud funny. But there's wisdom mixed with the wit."
—*The Orlando Sentinel*

Also by Clyde Edgerton
Published by Ballantine Books:

RANEY
WALKING ACROSS EGYPT
THE FLOATPLANE NOTEBOOKS
KILLER DILLER

IN MEMORY OF JUNIOR

Clyde Edgerton

BALLANTINE BOOKS • NEW YORK

All rights reserved under International and Pan-American Copyright Conventions. Published in the United States of America by Ballantine Books, a division of Random House, Inc., New York, and simultaneously in Canada by Random House of Canada Limited, Toronto.

This is a work of fiction. While, as in all fiction, the literary perceptions and insights are based on experience, all names, characters, places, and incidents are either products of the author's imagination or are used fictitiously. No reference to any real person is intended or should be inferred.

Thanks to O. Vic Miller, Phil Schlechty, W. C. Martin, Betty Foster, Clyde Yancey, and Harriett Purves.

Parts of this book originally appeared in slightly different form in *Frank*, *North Carolina Humanities*, and *Southern Exposure*.

Library of Congress Catalog Card Number: 92-15188

ISBN 0-345-38360-5

This edition published by arrangement with Algonquin Books of Chapel Hill, a division of Workman Publishing Company, Inc.

Manufactured in the United States of America

First Ballantine Books Edition: January 1994

For my mother,
Truma Warren Edgerton

The Bales and McCord Families

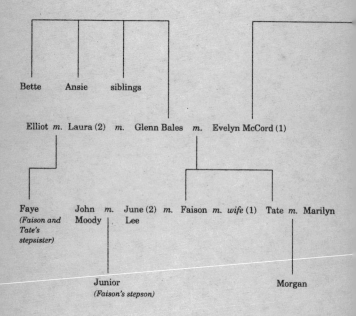

Bette   Ansie   siblings

Elliot *m.* Laura (2) *m.* Glenn Bales *m.* Evelyn McCord (1)

Faye   John *m.* June (2) *m.* Faison *m.* wife (1) Tate *m.* Marilyn
(Faison and Moody   Lee
Tate's
stepsister)

Junior   Morgan
(Faison's stepson)

siblings

wife (1) *m.* Grove McCord *m.* Tina (4)

wife (2)

wife (3)

Bobbie *m.* Adam
            (Four-eyes)

Others

Buster Douglas
truck driver

Gloria Palmer
*Glenn and Laura's
practical nurse*

Wilma and Harold Fuller
*Glenn and Laura's
neighbors*

Jimmy and Timmy Knight
Faison's neighbors, twins

Honour Walters

Anna Phillips
*Grove's childhood
sweetheart*

Bill Turpentine
gravedigger

Lamar Benfield
gravedigger

Fox Scerbo
*handyman, McGarren
Island*

Duck, Jo-Jo, and Melvin
Bill's friends

Part One

Truck Freight

1

Buster Douglas

I HAUL THINGS.

The footstone belonged to a Mr. Grove McCord. Old man. It was on the Cutler, Arkansas, to Summerlin, North Carolina, run. I was in on the deal from pickup to delivery because this new administration at Truck Freight Limited come in with this idea that if we don't specialize we'll be happier. So you pick up, you deliver, you forklift, you push paper. You do it all. Harebrained idea.

Take somebody like Yellow Freight, they specialize. In other words, if I'm working for them I either just drive, or just forklift, or just push paper. But at Limited I have to do it all, and it makes one big mess because you got all these people that won't hold up their end of the deal. If the idea worked it would be okay. It don't work. So I got my name in over at Yellow Freight, but don't nobody here know it.

Anyway, it so happened that this tombstone—footstone—pickup was *my* pickup and then it was on the tail end of my deliveries. To start of, this old man, this Mr. Grove McCord, calls in saying to meet him out at Shady Willows—the main cemetery in Cutler. Says he's got a footstone to be delivered, that he'll pay cash. So me and Ed drive out there and he's got this thing dismantled. There's the actual footstone itself, then this brass plate with his and his wife's names and birth dates and blanks for death dates on there, with all this fancy design work on it, and a little flower holder. He'd screwed the brass plate off the footstone, and the flower holder off the brass plate.

Me and Ed loaded it—got it up and just inside the back door of the trailer. No need to load it deeper.

He wants to ride with us to the station. No car, no nothing. So I ask him about his transportation and all, and he goes into this about by god, he'd always wanted to be buried in North Carolina anyway so he'd just got a buddy to take him on out to the graveyard and he'd dismantled the thing for shipment. He was going to take care of it all hisself, he said.

He had cash money. A roll of fifties and twenties.

We got to the station and packed the thing in a cardboard container and addressed it to a couple of his nephews in North Carolina. So. That was all that was left for him to do, he tells us, except get hisself back to

4

the BP station over on Huddle Road. Close to his house, I guess. Ed took him on out there.

Now all this so far is not such a big deal, but listen to this: he said what he had to do next was figure out how to get hisself to North Carolina, get a grave dug, get his nephews or somebody to help him set things up, get a white pine coffin delivered, *get in it, shoot hisself, and then get buried*. You figure it. This is what he said, and I didn't know whether to take him serious or not. I think he was just a old man off his rocker, see, so I didn't do nothing. But here's the thing.

I'd had something like six hours sleep in the last thirty-six when I started that haul. I got on the interstate and on in through Waynesville, stopping here and there, unloading stuff—rugs, collards, French doors—and headed for the final stop in Summerlin.

But see, being out of it from lack of sleep, I took a wrong turn somewhere west of Summerlin, and just as I was drifting off, the top of the damn trailer, going about, oh, forty mile an hour, hit some low-ass railroad bridge, if you can believe that. By that time, the footstone was the only thing left back there in the trailer. Way back at the back. When the top of the trailer jammed the bridge and flat stopped the truck, that footstone took off. There was this little pause and . . . a *whopawham*.

Part Two

I Wouldn't Tell This to Anybody

2

Gloria

MISS LAURA, SHE PROPPED UP IN THERE IN HER room on the pillows, leaning to the side a little. I go in and push her back up straight every once in a while. Mr. Glenn, he flat on his back in his room. His great big head look like a yellow salt lick somebody carved his face in. They both mighty sick. Have been, some time.

And you know all these white folk worked up because of *this* tension: whoever die first will mean who get this whole place. His boys—or her daughter.

The hospital won't take either one because you know how the hospitals are, and right now it look like Miss Laura she might actually be the first to pass, which would mean those boys would get the place. Cause Mr. Glenn and Miss Laura own the place joint ownership. At least that's the way I understand it.

And this place, the land—if it gets sold—will bring more money than would fill up heaven. Something like three, four million dollars is what they say. Land going eighty thousand dollars a acre round here. You believe that? My granddaddy would die again if he knowed that. He owned two acres. Bought them for something like thirty-five dollars a acre. And that was high back then.

Mr. Glenn and Miss Laura, they feel okay about each other. They always asking how the other one doing, except Miss Laura lately, she don't talk much no more. It's their families with the hard feelings—her daughter, his sons, his sisters.

Old Mr. and Mrs. Fuller, who is neighbors, *they visit*. Wilma and Harold. Lord have mercy. But cause of hard feelings in the family they don't visit both at the same time. They visit Mr. Glenn one day, and then Miss Laura the next.

This morning Mrs. Fuller was sitting in there at the foot of Miss Laura's bed. Mrs. Fuller dips snuff, and in her hand she carry about a dozen Kleenex tissues she use for a cuspidor, what do you call the word—portable?

And there sit Miss Laura's half-naked bird in his cage on a table next to the TV. Florida. What I want to know is who's going to get *him*. He be one poor, sick bird. I tried to tell Faye, that's Miss Laura's daughter, that he sick but she don't pay no mind. His feathers has come out all around his shoulders.

10

Faye is a little uppity, but okay all in all. Lawyer in Charlotte.

Miss Laura was propped up in her bed on some pillows while Mrs. Fuller was talking to her. I sit out in the hall where I can see she need anything. She sitting propped up there with her hair—a kind of dirty ocean color—piled up on her head. I don't have to move my chair more than three or four feet to see in Mr. Glenn's bedroom, then back to see in hers.

For Miss Laura, I think what goes on is mostly silent. When her daughter Faye put a hearing aid in her ear, she by golly pull it out, and has throwed it away twice. I found it in the trash can both times.

I had a load of wash in, so I sat there and listened to Mrs. Fuller talking. Nobody don't pay me much mind, unless one of them need the pot or something. Registered nurse from social services come in every few days. A teenager spend the night. Course I have to bathe them, feed them, all that stuff, but I been practical nursing all my life. I got started early and so far I always found this kind of work around here. People know about me. I already got myself lined up with Miss Ivy Terrell if she happen to outlast Mr. Glenn and Miss Laura. Sometimes it's hard work, and what I wonder about, I wonder who'll do it for me if'n I get in such a fix. I wonder about that a lot. I hope I go fast when the Lord call *me* home.

See, Miss Laura won't Mr. Glenn's first wife.

A woman named Evelyn was. I do remember. See, Evelyn run off and left Mr. Glenn with those two boys of his. She was still nursing the youngest, Tate. It was all kind of a unusual thing. Mr. Glenn, he could tell

11

you about the leaving better than I could. Course he don't talk too much anymore now that he so sick.

Glenn

I can remember.

I was burning up with hate, driving up that long driveway with them in the car, and looking way ahead up there at the front porch for Mama. I dreaded, really dreaded, facing her.

I was burning up with hate.

Tate was laying there beside me on the seat, smelling rich, crying. I didn't have no idea what to do with him.

I didn't want to face Mama.

Evelyn just walked out on us, see, and I hated her— for my sake, for Tate's sake, and for Faison's sake, too. They were too little to know what she had done to them. To all three of us.

I could see Faison in the rearview mirror—sitting back there in the backseat with his arms folded. Had on a T-shirt with catsup down the front.

She'd stood there in the kitchen that same morning at three o'clock, stood there and said she was leaving, said that there was no choice but to leave. That she was *sorry*. I moved around the kitchen table while she talked, while she stood there in the hall door and talked to me. I was walking a foot above the floor it seemed like and when my hand fell on something, like the table, the table was gone. The whole inside of the kitchen, the house, had gone away, had whited out, except for her face, her mouth moving, saying all those words. She said things about Mama and Papa that I never thought a person would even *think* about anybody, much less them.

Listen. Tate was at her breast. She left him while he was at her breast—a baby. A little baby boy sucking on her titty when she walked off and left him behind.

I wouldn't tell this to anybody.

Mama was sitting there on the porch shelling peas. I could see her in her chair.

I saw Bette in the yard, beside the house, heading around back.

See, Evelyn had not been loving me when I thought she had. That was the only answer. She had been fooling me. There must have been something deep and bad wrong with her all along from the beginning. Some secret thing. She had fell in to the Devil. There's no doubt about it.

Then, of course, along came Laura. And she's been so good to me. So good. I don't know what I would have done without her.

Bette

I was outside when Glenn come driving up that driveway. I knew it was a unusual time of day, late morning, for him to be driving up. Normally he'd just walk from across the back field.

I noticed he was driving a little fast. The car was swerving some. Dust was kicking up.

What I done was start for the back of the house so I could go on around and come up on the other side and look and listen through the holly bush because I figured something won't right. I never have minded listening in when I thought something won't right. I've been able to offer help because of it, too.

I got around there about time he stopped the car under the middle oak. It was a warm morning, summertime. Later that day it stormed. I remember.

Mama kept right on shelling peas. Mama would have shelled peas through a tornado. Sitting there looking down at the peas, then looking up at that car, never moving her head, then back down at the peas, through them little round wire-frame glasses. I was right up against the holly bush.

Course Mama knew who it was. She knew everybody's car. She must have known something was wrong, too—him driving up of a morning, on a weekday.

When the car stopped, dust drifted up around it and on over toward the well shed. I can see it now. Little Faison jumped out and started running. He always did like to go out down behind the house and look at the pigs.

Glenn stood there behind the car, holding Tate out and away from him—like something, you know, infected or something. Then it looked like it took him a year to come on over to the porch to talk to Mama. You could see it on his face, that the words were inside him, about to get out. They fell out about the time he got to Mama's feet. He said, "Evelyn left, Mama."

Mama kept shelling peas. That was Mama. She looked at him and then back down, picked out a pea—a bad one—and dropped it in with the hulls.

I thought to myself, Well, I will be *damned*. And I never cuss. Pretty Evelyn. What could have led her off into something she would have to answer for on Judgment Day? And I could feel Mama thinking the same thing. And poor Glenn. He looked like he was standing there lost forever, holding that baby. I felt so sorry for him.

"She what?" said Mama.

"Left."

"I was afraid of it," Mama says. "But I never thought it would be with a baby at her titty. I swanee."

"Mama, she just left and I . . . I hadn't even been to work yet."

"Give him here." She put her peas down. "Get to work," she says. "We'll figure something out. Just go ahead to work." She took the baby. "You supposed to already be on the road, ain't you?"

"Yes ma'am."

"Lord, he smells," said Mama. "Go call Bette. She's out back, I think." Then she said that we could use some more hands around there. That Faison was old enough to cut out them row ends that needed it. That he could get right on that.

I started back around to the back, and sure enough, Faison was out there looking at the pigs.

After that Mama acted like she'd known all along. And I'd say she had. She'd seen Evelyn's set of playing cards, asked Glenn about them. Mama could always judge character. And she'd tell you she could. Because she could. That afternoon Mama's exact words were, "I knew her when I met her. I knew and should have said more than I did." She thought right off that that Grove, that Grove McCord—Evelyn's brother— probably had something to do with her leaving. Course, when I found out why she *did* leave, or what I heard, I was sick to my stomach, except nobody else ever found out. As far as I know.

Evelyn

I married Glenn with open eyes, glazed with romance of some sort. Here was a boy who was a salesman, yet had a house on the farm. He was going nowhere but up, and after a few years on the farm, we'd move to town. That was the plan.

"Well, honey, welcome to the farm," Glenn's mother

had said. "It's not a easy life, but you'll get used to it." Why would she say that? She knew I had grown up on a farm. But if I'd said, "Mrs. Bales, you know I grew up on a farm," she would have looked at me and said, "Why, what on earth are you talking about?" Do you see? She ran the edge of the field called irritation, dishonesty, poking fun, ran it so lightly it was invisible to the people in her camp. If you stand up to it, it's denied. And she skirted the edge so close she could, I imagine, always hide any justified guilt from her own eyes and heart. I hate that kind of attitude. She was always behind it, peering over, and I grew to dislike her more the longer I knew her.

I knew what to do on a farm. I could churn, can vegetables, sew. I could even plow, and Bette or Ansie, Glenn's sisters, wouldn't have been caught dead plowing.

But before we got settled good, the baby came. Faison.

Glenn seemed always gone to Wadesboro or Salisbury, selling vacuum cleaners. And I finally came to realize that he wasn't interested in moving to town. He wouldn't leave home. That homeplace. And the way my sisters-in-law and mother-in-law helped me was to tell me what I was doing wrong, and how I was doing it wrong. They were always available to do that, and they were there on earth to worship and obey God and Papa Bales. And Mr. Bales—Papa Bales—and all those uncles knew in their blood that their job on earth was to order and demand service from women, land, children, and animals. And all the aunts had, as far as I know, once their baby eyes opened and focused, quickly learned to accept—even covet—being ordered, if not by men themselves directly, then by the habits and needs of men and men's work on the land. These were just facts—like trees.

The old man was always out in the field or in a barn or in town, except when he was inside eating or sleeping. I don't feel exactly right getting into all of this, but let me tell you: he smelled like sour sweat, except on Sunday after the Saturday-night bath—in the winter. And in the summer, Thursday too, after the Wednesday-night bath. It was a smell that I honestly think Glenn learned to revere somehow.

The two of them, Mr. and Mrs. Bales, were as set in their ways as stumps. They had learned to survive like ants, foxes, rabbits making their appointed rounds. They didn't have time to develop new tactics, plans, or ideas that weren't in their blood when they were born or passed down to them to live by, to stay alive by. It was on account in part, I have to say, of their always having to dig for a living. Scrape, skimp, save, and store away for winter. I got to where I couldn't bear the thought of living there on that place until I died. With them always there. Every day. Monday through Monday, January through January.

Glenn's daddy did have this one little story, this one little springtime observation: a little baby robin when it is first born looks like an old dog's red peter. That was the humor, the poetry in the family's life. And none of them ever went to a fall dance—or any dance—because they were Baptists. And Glenn was a baby. Such a baby.

Gloria

So, Mrs. Fuller, sitting there at the foot of Miss Laura's bed, she start in with that story about what happened to that little boy of Faison's. Faison's stepson. Mr. Fuller, he sitting there beside Mrs. Fuller turning that baseball cap in his hands and looking out the window. That's his customary pose. Every once in a while his eyelids droop down. He tickles me. He'll sit there and nod off, jerk up his head, nod off, jerk up, nod off.

Mrs. Fuller, she went on and on like she always does. Every once in a while she spit into that handful of Kleenex. Sometimes Miss Laura she act like she hear her, but I don't think she do. Miss Laura be leaning to the side a little, looking back and forth from Mr. Fuller to Mrs. Fuller, then at that bird, who be walking around in his cage, shivering, dragging his tail. He usually don't even walk. But when Mrs. Fuller get to talking, sometimes he walk around, shiver, drag his tail.

Mrs. Fuller had done told Miss Laura twice about the tombstone—the little boy's—I know, cause I heard it, sitting right here in this hall. But sometimes she get a new detail mixed in, and I like to hear her talk, no matter.

So Mrs. Fuller go on and on, bringing that handful of Kleenex up to her mouth every now and then. I do declare I believe I'd use a little jar myself if I was going to dip at a neighbor's house. She go right at it—telling the story—like Miss Laura can hear her, which maybe she can, but I doubt it. I have to pure-t yell at her sometimes. Real loud: *Miss Laura, git yo ass on the pot.*

Wilma Fuller

"Tate's been the most sensible of the two, even though they both been ugly. At least that's my notion. And thank goodness he had enough sense to go to college and then teach on the college level. The high schools is pure bedlam these days. Of course Tate hadn't had to go through a real tragedy like Faison has. And it was such a tragedy. Such a tragedy. I know I told you but you just don't remember, Miss Laura.

"See, June Lee . . . No ma'am, *June Lee*—Faison's wife—had been going to Preacher Gordon for counseling a good, oh, two months when the car wreck happened. Lord, lord. Such an awful tragedy. I guess she had been a member of the church for almost a year. Then found out she needed some counseling—what with her divorce from that John Moody and child custody and all that.

"You know, people didn't used to get divorced."

I'm telling all this to Miss Laura again. She forgets real easy. But it's about her family, even if it was stepfamily. A family is a family. She needs to know, to keep up. And somebody has to tell her. "Anyway, Mary

Bowden says she'd seen them go shopping together at some point way back. Her and Faison. Before she got her divorce from the Moody boy and married Faison.

"It's good she was going to Preacher Gordon on a regular basis when the wreck happened because it was natural for her to keep the visits up regular, you know, just to come on over and see him on her next scheduled visit. And he's still got a full schedule on Monday mornings—and Thursday nights, too, which a lot of people don't know about. He has to do it at night because so many people work now, full time, in the day. Women.

"Harold, close that blind so the sun won't get in Miss Laura's eyes . . . There, that's better. We can more or less tell who's coming to see Preacher Gordon because he'll drop in on the circle meeting and say something like so-and-so might could use a little visit from somebody, and we'll know so-and-so has been in to see him about some worry of hers, and so one of us'll drop in to visit her that week. And there are ones he don't mention, too. He knows which ones to mention.

"Anyway, we was stopped at the intersection of the expressway and, ah . . . What road was that, Harold? Redmill? Or Arcadia?"

"Redmill."

Harold *will* go to sleep on you.

"Redmill Road, no more than a minute before the wreck, when she come barreling through there with that boy in the backseat leaning way up forward with his hands on the back of the front seat, sort of holding on. Didn't have a shirt on, and you could see dirt rings around his neck. She was trying to make the light. If

21

we hadn't been turning to go to the mall we would have come up on the wreck, sure as the world.''

"He was dead before he hit the ground. Flew fi'ty-one feet.''

"Harold. Miss Laura don't want to be hearing about that.''

"Took off both ears.''

"Harold.''

"She just had the one broke rib and a bump—''

"I don't think—''

"That's what Drew said.''

"Harold . . . Well anyway, Miss Laura, the thing about it is, nobody knew what was going on behind the scenes about the tombstone business until Preacher Gordon sort of, I guess, verified the facts behind it all. Told Graham Fisher, and then too, Mary—two doors down from where Faison and June Lee lived, you now—kind of pieced it all together. She said Faison spent the night over there several times before they got married and I *think* before she got divorced—or at least stayed real, real late. Don't surprise me a bit in this day and age. Faison's got one of them camouflage trucks. Course you probably knew that. Did you know he had one of them camouflage trucks, Miss Laura?'' She can't half hear.

"Well he does. And lord a mercy—how anybody could live in a motel is something I don't know, either. How he can afford it. I mean, it's a very cheap motel, but I still don't know how he can afford it—with the kind of work he does, moving houses. Twenty dollars a night—that's what, six hundred dollars a month?''

"He rented a house.''

"That's right. He did rent a house."

Harold's sitting there twirling that ball cap in his hand. He'll wear it anywhere. He tried to wear it to church twicet.

"Anyway, Mary says Faison was good to that boy. But I don't think he's much of a house mover. When do you see a house getting moved around here? Of course I guess he travels around doing it, and you're just not that aware of it. Did you ever get to hear the whole story about the tombstone thing, Miss Laura—the little boy's tombstone? You know, what broke them up. You been so sick. Did you ever hear it, Miss Laura?" Deaf as a cabbage.

"Near as I can tell, the little boy's name was John Moody, Junior, after June Lee's *first* husband. But she'd had such a rough time of it with John Senior, she promised Faison that as soon as they got married she would change the little boy's name to Faison Bales, Junior. Legally. They were just calling the boy Junior, irregardless, anyway.

"Well, the first thing Preacher Gordon thought about when she told him about the name change was how the *boy* felt about it, because he says he—Preacher Gordon—thought changing a little boy's name was a kind of critical thing to do unless the little boy was one hundred percent in favor of it. He asked her to bring in the boy. She did, and the boy said he *wanted* his name changed. So Preacher Gordon counseled him a little bit, you know, but the little boy stayed all in favor of it."

"Faison's got a camouflage boat, too," said Harold. "Took the boy fishing some."

"Preacher Gordon says he thought there might be

23

some legal problem with calling somebody a junior after somebody who was their stepfather, but of course he never got around to checking into that before the poor little boy was stone dead and I don't know what the law might be on that."

"I think you can name them whatever you want to."

"Well, I don't think so, Harold. Then after the burial service—he won't but eleven or twelve, poor thing—after the burial service, Faison and her, June Lee, had started walking back toward the family car when he looked down on the little nameplate that they had stuck in the ground for the gravediggers, I guess, and he pulled her over there and started giving her down the country. That's what Celia Joyner told Mary. Can you imagine that—at a funeral?

"But you know, Miss Laura, Faison's problems, his whole general attitude, is bound to stem from them boys being left by their mama like they was. Bound to.

"Anyway, there at the burial service, I was too far in back of the crowd to hear anything, but I saw him holding her by the arm and pointing down to the ground talking about something. I thought it had something to do with the flowers and didn't pay that much attention to it. You didn't either, did you, Harold?"

"I wadn't there."

"That's right. You stayed home. But Mary did have to call the sheriff out there to their house to break up a fight a few days after that. Said they fought across the backyard and into the garage—like dogs. Idn't that awful? They were fighting about the name—about what name was going on the tombstone. Mary heard them.

"After that fight is when she started in to see the

24

preacher sometimes *more* than once a week. Once it was twicet in the same day. At the time, I didn't know whether to say anything to Preacher Gordon or not, you know, about whether I ought to visit. She had a couple of friends in the church—that Watkins girl, and Sheila Peterson talked to her sometimes—so I didn't say anything. Course I ain't known Faison Bales to set foot in a church since he was a boy. And I don't imagine you have either. I don't understand how they change so.

"Well, right many people got interested in what the tombstone would say on it. Claremont done it. And they are . . . slow. It was right big, not too thick, and dark. Dark gray. People had got interested enough, you know, to want to see what was written on it. On the stone. What name they used. First off they didn't bury him in the Bales section, they buried him in some neutral site out there amongst that little clump of trees where there ain't ever been no graves because of the roots. But they got root cutters now just like they've got everything else under the sun we don't need. Well, anyway, there it was: John Moody, Junior, 1978-1989.

"Then it wadn't more than two days passed when here comes Mary telling me there's a *foot*stone out there, a light pink one, in *place* of the tombstone. The tombstone had been *removed*.

"Me and Harold drove out to take a look. Course we didn't get out of the car—you could drive right up to it and read it without getting out. Sure enough, it said Faison Bales, Junior, with the dates. The grave was still red and fresh. The tombstone at the head was gone and there was that pink footstone at the foot. Mary says he hauled that thing out there in his truck hisself, and

25

switched them. When I saw that name, Faison Bales, Junior, I knew it won't right. I could feel it. That boy ought to be named after his blood daddy . . . Ma'am? What did she say, Harold?''

"She said, 'Where was they *going?* ' "

"Where was who going? Where was who going, Miss Laura? . . . Oh, the little boy and his mama. When they had the wreck, you mean. Well, I don't know as anybody knows. She was in a hurry was all I could tell. She was going *away* from the mall. Mary did say she'd just had a argument with Faison and had pulled that boy out of the house by his arm. Then barreling through that intersection going too fast, and that boy sitting up on the edge of the backseat with his shirt off and dirt rings around his neck. It was a yellow car. If he'd been wearing a seat belt that might have saved his life. Of course the car could have caught on fire and then both of them could have got all hung up in there and burned up.''

"She was wearing hers," said Harold.

"Oh, I didn't know that."

"Yep. That's what Drew said—up at the rescue squad. What I don't understand is why they don't make you wear seat belts in a bus. If they're so safe. You can get thrown forty foot in a bus and still be in there."

"What does that have to do with anything, Harold?"

"Them seats and poles and stuff in there is *hard*."

"Well, anyway, I've never heard anything up to it. She quit coming to church and to see Preacher Gordon.

"And that house that Faison was moving, out on Lake Collier Road, has been sitting there on them blocks with that truck hooked to it, lord, for . . . how long, Harold?''

"Month or two."

"Month or two.

"Course you know I would have thought she'd have changed that footstone back by now. It's been well over a year . . . What's that, Miss Laura? What? What did she say, Harold?''

"She says she wants a pink footstone, too."

"You tell Faye, Miss Laura. You tell Faye. I think you're already set.''

"Maybe she can get the boy's, after it's changed again.''

"Harold."

"Well, all they'd have to do was turn it over and put her name on top.''

"Harold!"

"Ain't that right, Miss Laura. You wouldn't mind having a used footstone, would you?''

Harold gets right ridiculous sometimes. Showing off. ''Har—''

"Look, she's laughing."

"It's not funny, Harold. Miss Laura ain't going to have a secondhand footstone. Are you, Miss Laura? No sirree. Speaking of that, me and Harold got to pick out ours one of these days. It's something you can't do too early. But. We got to be getting on now. Lord, we been sitting here over an hour. It's good to see you sitting up again, Miss Laura, and you tell Faye we come by to see you. Harold, go out to the car and get that little pretty we brought Miss Laura. I forgot it.''

Harold's knees pop evertime he stands up. And he's

got so he limps. And hisses at that bird like some teen-ager. Harold's a something.

"Harold is just a joker, Miss Laura. Don't you pay no attention to him. Here, let me push you back up straight. You got to leaning a little bit there. Why, you're liable to be around longer than any of us . . . Ma'am? . . . No, Harold is in lectronics. He's got a lectronics shop. You know that, Miss Laura . . . No, he don't make tombstones. It's Claremont made that footstone, the pink one. They're the only one does pink ones, I think. Here. Here comes Harold with a little box of something for you—I know how much you like it—and you keep that smile on your face, and keep sitting up. We'll be seeing you—and Preacher Gordon ought to be by sometime soon."

Gloria

I was sitting in the kitchen, eating my afternoon sandwich, when they passed through, headed out.

"How's *Mr.* Bales?" Mrs. Fuller ask me.

"He bout the same," I say. "He asleep now. Been bothered with the bedsores some."

Miss Wilma looked around, checked out the kitchen. She *will* check up on you. It was clean and straight. The kitchen is one thing I always keep straight. That

28

teenager that spends the night leaves crumbs and dishes sometimes.

"Well, we'll be back to see him before too long," she said. What she always say.

See, way back, Mr. Glenn he got sick and Miss Laura she took care of him for years and years, and then she got sick, too, and that's when I come to work, in the daytimes, mostly. That teenager come in at night. But she don't have to do much but baby-sit. They fired two for not looking in on them like they ought to.

When Miss Laura's daughter, Faye, come from Charlotte for a day or two, me and the night girl both get off. Faye come most weekends.

Them boys don't visit their daddy like they ought to. I don't care what the reason—but then, too, my chiren don't visit me neither. Nobody's chiren visit much anymore. It's a bad sign about the times.

But I'll tell you this. I've seen days I could choke them everone—I'm talking about *these* people. They so *picky*. You know what I mean? But then, too, there been days I wished I was white and everything wouldn't be so hard, but most time I realize if I was white how much I'd miss out on.

Mr. and Mrs. Fuller they sit down and talk to me sometimes. They right nice. Course they talk to anybody.

See, they reasons that if Miss Laura die first, which had always seemed very unlikely, then when Mr. Glenn die, the homeplace *would* go to the boys, and none of it to Mr. Glenn's sisters—that's Miss Bette and Miss Ansie—who have raised the boys, and who, word is, figure they deserve at least some of the homeplace, being as they worked the land all their lives and raised the boys. It would go to the boys because Mr. Glenn, they say, won't leave no will because he think that would hurt somebody's feelings. It's right complicated and I don't try too hard to understand it because it ain't none of my bidness.

Course this is just my surmising from what all Mr. and Mrs. Fuller say, but mostly I think they visit because they got good hearts. They do surmise a good bit though. Specially Miss Wilma. She really do. She surmise a *lot*. But you can't say she ain't good to Miss Laura.

Laura

I open the box and look over the different shapes of chocolate. Whitman's Sampler. My very favorite! Yes sir! My very favorite!

I always was blessed with good neighbors.

The first piece of warm chocolate candy is that boy, Faison. I swallow him—the one always stuck his tongue out at me, cussed me even. Then run away at sixteen— stole Glenn's truck with the wood saw in the back—to stay with that Grove McCord, Evelyn's brother, and ended up no-count at all.

I finger another little hunk of chocolate, with a nut

of some sort in it, I bet. I eat it. Oh, it's got a crunch. It's that Grove McCord. And who—Harold?—said he heard he's coming back here to *die*? Somebody heard it. Nobody wants him back here.

I eat that other boy, Tate, that ran from me, wouldn't mind a thing I said. At least he went to college.

A lumpy piece. Evelyn. The one that left Glenn. I eat her. She deserted those boys.

Now, that awful Grove, Evelyn's brother. Did I just eat him? I'll eat him again. This is good candy! My very favorite!

Then I lick a pretty little piece, a piece that is my warm daughter, Faye. Born of Elliot. Sometimes I wish so hard that Elliot had lived. Sometimes I wish so hard. My Faye takes care of me, pays for the nurse, won't put me in no nursing home, stands between me and the whole black ocean full of snakes and alligators and those two ugly, mean boys. Glenn can't do nothing for me no more. Lord, he's worse off than ever and I can't help him. I'll eat him in a minute. I lord spent every ounce of energy I had left in the whole world tending to him all those years and bless Faye, she was right to insist on that joint ownership of this farm. I said it didn't make any difference. She said it did. She knew what was right. So that I don't get left out in the cold when all is said and done.

Oh, my, I remember the times Glenn fell in the bathroom and I couldn't get him up and had to go call them boys and not one word of thanks from anybody. Those sisters of his have everything. They have health and they complain all the time. I never complained once in my life—changing his diapers, standing him up in his slippers, feeding him.

I lick Faye until there's not much left of her. Then I eat her. She'll get the homeplace. I'll outlive him. I've *got* to. I eat the nurse, Gloria, next. She's short with me sometimes. I eat one of these little tiny pieces wrapped in gold aluminum foil—Florida. Poor thing. I eat poor Florida.

I look over the piece that is my poor sick husband, Glenn. Faye—did I eat her?—Faye kept saying, Take him to a rest home, Mama, and I finally did but lord, lord, he cried and cried with his hands on top of his head before I even took him out of the car and I couldn't stand it, and Faye won't ever understand until she has to face the same thing. If she does. I hope she don't. But if she does, she'll bring whoever it is back home, too.

Glenn. I eat him.

I can't think of anybody else to eat except my Sunday school class. But they all look like the same one: Mrs. Loftis-Barnes-Poole-Tinkner-Smith-Darnell-Simpson-Rhymer. I eat her. Then I eat the church choir—all the rest of the candy, piece by piece. The sopranos, basses, those others. It makes me warm.

I always believed, in secret, that as soon as I married him I could wean him from his family. But it never worked. The more I tried to wean him the more glued to them he got. There was something about them all that was so . . . so close it didn't make sense. I came to realize, see, that Glenn would jump up on a horse and run after any one of them—his mama, papa, sisters, brothers, with them on a runaway horse and him trying to save them, while I was sinking in quicksand, calling out to him, Glenn, Glenn, save me, I'm sinking. His eyes would have been back over his shoulder, looking at me, but he would be galloping full steam after any one of the others. I decided to love him anyway, because he was Glenn. And his gift to me was that joint ownership, and that was because I'd worked to the bone taking care of him, because those boys had turned out so bad, so much against me, so cold-shouldered, because their mama run off, especially that Faison, and everybody knew how it was—how much work I put in—so that if Glenn had left anything to those sisters and those boys, then there would have been talk, and I know that if there was anything Glenn feared and dreaded all his life, it was talk of family discord, disharmony. That fear was something he ate every day. It was sticky and he ate it just about every day—that fear of discord and disharmony. Why did Glenn do that? Discord and disharmony could have been fresh, like lemon.

I do wish I wasn't sick, but I love my candy.

3

Harold Fuller

TATE WAS ABOUT TO GET INTO HIS NEW AIRPLANE TO
ferry the seller home—fellow named Pillner, I think—
when we heard the crash at the Mount Station bridge.
Had to be a truck. It happens about once a year. They
need to dig out that road some more. Then we heard a
little aftershock—a little thump after the crash. I asked
Drew about it next day and he said somebody called it
in on a car phone that a truck had hit the bridge out
there, but when they got out there they'd left the scene.

The reason I was at the airfield was to see Tate's new
little airplane. It was a airplane just like Grove—his
Uncle Grove—used to have and I think that's part of

why he wanted one. The boys—Faison and Tate—have always been crazy about their Uncle Grove. He used to come through on his truck runs and they'd meet him somewhere. Then Faison—at some point, I don't remember exactly—run off and lived with Grove. Tate was still right little when that happened.

He's a interesting young man, Tate is. Good boy. Had some hard times. He says he's hoping to put a little airstrip out on the homeplace—across that back field—so he won't have so far to drive when he wants to fly.

This flying thing. The whole family on Grove and Evelyn's side has had this airplane thing for as far back as I can remember. Albert Copeland, their cousin, tried to build a floatplane for, I don't know, twenty years or more, finally got one to fly—and still flies it. And one of Albert's boys was in the air force. No, let's see. That was his sister's boy. Tate went in the navy when that one went in the air force. Albert's boy is the one lost a arm and leg—was in the marines, I think.

But you see, Grove, like I say, was Albert's cousin—let's see, Grove was Albert's daddy's sister's boy I believe. I don't remember her name. His was Tyree. Anyway, Grove was flying before Albert ever started. It was like it was in their blood, you know what I mean. And it kind of sifted on down to the younger ones—or some of them. There's another one over the other side of Draughn flies acrobatics, loop de loops.

But listen. Grove . . . Grove—way back then—was flying off a *pole*. Damnedest thing you ever seen. It was '46, or maybe '47, and Grove got this idea. See, he ended up with a new airplane and a little piece of land out by the lake. He'd said he could get a little bit of land and a nice new airplane, or he could get a lot of land—enough for a runway—and a used airplane. Income from hauling liquor, you know, bootlegging. He opted for the new airplane. Little bit of land. Not enough for a runway. So he had to build this pole thing. This was right after the war, I guess right around the time Evelyn left.

Anyway, Grove got a load of pilings—this is true—pilings that ferries run up against, and tied them together with steel cable. Half buried, half above ground. There's no telling where they come from. I think he had about nine of them wired together with this steel cable around the outside, three of them with a little more height sticking up out the middle, and a swivel and another cable, a long single cable, to hook to the tip of the airplane wing, see. He'd start his ground roll going in a circle like a mule around a cider press, you know, gain speed and gain speed. After rolling a few hundred feet, he'd clear the ground, gain speed, and then of course he'd rigged this release mechanism modeled after that carrier catapult release that Barn Poteet—lives in Fuquay-Varina—actually designed for the navy. A lot of people don't know that. A mechanism that a certain pound pull, you know, would separate, shaped like this. And if it didn't work, there was a handle in the cockpit he could pull and there you'd go. Off in the wild blue yonder. Yeah, he was a something. And I don't think that mechanism failed once. Well, I know it didn't. And when he wore a deep enough circle in the grass, he'd lengthen or shorten the cable. I always waited for the day the cable might catch and start winding around them pilings and wind him right on into hisself more or less, but it never happened.

I liked old Grove, a real likable fellow as long as you was on his right side, and I liked to hang around out there when I could, over there, and over here at Hollis Field, too. Course all that's long gone, where Grove flew off that pole. TechComm Commons has took it all over. Sha, nothing new about that. I understand they got Japs and Arabs and no telling who-all buying land out there.

Grove—Grove was a wiry man, tall, worked in shorts in the summer, which was odd back then, for a man, or for a woman, far as that goes. And he kept his hair real short over his ears, almost shaved. And he'd wing that thing off the pole like a slingshot. It was a new airplane, like I said.

Wouldn't nobody fly off the pole but Grove. And I can remember him talking about how to do it—the mechanics of it, the touch you used and all. Oh, he'd rigged up the wing, too. You know, to take the strain. He was a kind of legend there for a while. Married several times.

I used to fly with him to Ocracoke and Portsmouth—when the village was still out there at Portsmouth. There was a little grass landing strip. He'd pick me up here at Hollis Field. I never did fly with him off the pole, though.

He called his business Grove's Sky Ferry. Didn't last long.

Tate's been out of flying a right long time, so when he got a notion to get back in it, I told him I knew everybody out there at Hollis—Coach, Gary, all them—

and that I'd introduce him and all that, so that's what I did, and so on the day this fellow flew his plane in, I was out there when he closed the deal.

It was a little unusual, him deciding all of a sudden to get back into flying, but I figure it's also part because of his son. That boy is a sight—a downright disgrace. Long hair, earring, the works. I figure Tate felt like he wanted to get the boy interested in something, something they could maybe do together since him and his wife split up. Marilyn. That was her name. Another oddball.

Of course, Faison, you know, lost his stepson. That was a shame. Damn shame. But Tate, he's come a long way under the circumstances. He went on to college and made something of hisself. Earns a good salary out at the college, probably. Got into this psychology stuff. And was actually in the war, a hero. He won a big medal, a Silver Something, I think. Been me, I'd a made a career out of it—the navy.

Grove sent him a white scarf, and Tate took it to the navy with him and on all his missions. They had that in the newspaper.

So I was out there at Hollis Field with him and we waited for the plane to fly in, the one he wanted to buy, did buy. It's a tail-dragger. A '46 Super Cruiser. Fabric covered. Just like the one Grove used to have back when.

Tate and the seller, fellow named, what did I say? Pilsner? Or Pillner? Jim Pilsner, I believe—I can't remember—and some more of us were sitting together in the flight shack, talking. Gary had checked out the engine and airframe. Coach had flown it. Said it flew like a dream. Tate had flown it. I could tell he knew he ought to hide his enthusiasm until the deal was made.

It was time for somebody to make a move.

"Jim, could we walk outside a minute?" Tate said. Sitting there, kind of eager.

"Sure," says Jim. Jumped right up.

So they went on out and started walking toward that little airplane, sitting there—pretty. Just as pretty and sweet as she could be.

Tate had told me about his plan. He was going to offer eleven, then finally eleven-five, then back out of the deal if the man didn't drop his price—which was twelve-five.

Well, I was watching through the window there and they said three or four words and shook hands. I couldn't figure it. What happened, Tate told me later, was that he offered the guy eleven, the guy said no, Tate looked at the plane— big mistake—and said, Okay, twelve-five.

Whether or not he can get that boy of his interested in it remains to be seen. Tate didn't *say* that's why he bought the airplane, but I just figured that might be part of it.

Mom took me over to Dad's this afternoon and tonight I ended up coming back to Mom's. I didn't want
to go to the ball game in the first place, but he meets
me at the bottom of the stairs at his place, his apartment—Mom got the house in the settlement—and he
tells me first that he just bought an airplane like he's
been showing me pictures of. I said great. I mean it's
neat, but I'm not flipped out over it or anything. Then
he wanted to know if I wanted to go see the Bulls play
baseball. I guess I shrugged. He's got this thing about
taking me places. Like that's supposed to solve some
kind of problem.

He's also got this thing about my hair and stuff, but
he won't come out with it. He like accepts it—or something—and hates it at the same time. Something like
that. He keeps saying he thought long hair went out a
long time ago. Like that's supposed to make some kind
of difference.

So I went on up to my room, put up my gym bag,
and got on the computer for some Tetris. I've got a
pretty neat room over there, actually. Some posters and
stuff. I keep my CDs in both places.

He was downstairs, outside, probably arguing with
Mom about something. Then he comes up and stands
in my door for a minute. I can feel him standing there
and he says, "I figured maybe we could fly down to
Ocracoke one day for lunch since I've got the plane
now."

He's been showing me these pictures of this airplane his uncle used to fly. So now he's got one. He like worships this uncle who I met one time when I was about three. This old guy used to fly airplanes and drive trucks and all this, but he's about a hundred years old now. He's the reason Dad started flying in the first place and everything. That's what Dad said. There are all these cousins of his—ours—who flew airplanes, float-planes, and stuff. Some of them never got a pilot's license. Which Mom couldn't believe.

"You think you'd want to do that?" he says.

"Yeah, probably so." I was like already into the Tetris and he was wanting to discuss this hypothetical venture.

"How about a Bulls game tonight?"

"Not especially." My damn voice is changing, squeak and thunder. Freaks me out. Strange, man.

"Well, I'd like for you to go."

"I'd like to do this now." He and Mom know exactly how to bug me.

"I'm not talking about now," he says. "I'm talking about tonight."

So we're in the third-base bleachers. We get there early and the groundskeepers are still out there working on the infield. Okay? So I'm wearing my cutoff jeans, silver earring, the black beret, and my Doc Martins. That's what I like to wear. That's what I'm most comfortable in.

Baseball like as far as I'm concerned is about as boring as it gets. Dad sits there and he says if you *know the game* it's exciting because something is always going on that's full of like *drama* and stuff like that. I mean.

He says, "They used to pack the dirt extra tight between first base and second for Maury Wills when the Dodgers were playing at home." He's told me this at least twenty times. So Maury Wills could have extra traction while stealing second. All that.

I chewed my pizza, looked straight ahead at the guy spraying water from a hose. Big-deal excitement.

When the national anthem started, and we stood up, I didn't even think about it—I left my beret on.

"Son, take off your hat," he says.

I swear I'd forgotten, but I'm having problems with his tone of voice, so I don't respond.

"Take off that hat," he hisses. Venom.

I step away from him like man, like *what* is going on here? There is no law about hat-wearing as far as I know.

He went for the hat. I ducked, threw up my arms. He grabbed the hat. I held it to my head, lost my footing, gave up the hat, then moved away—and *kept* moving, right on down the bleacher steps among all these fans standing at attention singing their little hearts out. I didn't stop walking until I was home at Mom's. I mean like what is the big deal? You tell me.

I picked up the phone upstairs when he finally called. I imagine he waited around after the game was over, then went on home. I listened in.

"Hello, Marilyn? Is Morgan there?"

"He's upstairs."

"Can I speak to him?"

"I think he's absorbed in something at the moment."

"Well, then tell him I waited for him for a good while and that—no, don't tell him anything. I'll try to talk to him later."

"What did you do?"

"What did *I* do? Marilyn, I asked him to take his hat off for the national anthem. That's what I asked him to do."

"He said you yelled at him."

"Oh. Well, listen, Marilyn . . . for god's sake, Marilyn."

I asked Mom one time why they got married and all. Don't get me wrong, he's my dad and everything. He's all right. We've done some fun things. She said he told her a story about when he won his medal in Vietnam—his big-deal Silver Star—and it "broke her heart" and that's when she decided to marry him. So I don't know why the hell he won't tell me. Then maybe *I'd* feel like marrying him or something. He won't tell it to me, probably never will. I'm not *old* enough, he said. It must be a hell of a story, but I'm not holding my breath. Then, so fine, he's a hero.

One of the things that ripped Mom up was he tried to give me this shotgun for Christmas three years ago, when I was thirteen. She flipped right out. And of course I don't want a gun.

And boy does Mom hate Uncle Faison. She used to talk and talk about these sucking noises he made on his toothpick. She'd say stuff like, "Can't he get it through his head that those noises *make noises*."

Mom was big on me getting into computers, following my intellectual bent, as she puts it. She's planning to stay around here, so I'm more or less stuck here until

I can get off to college. I'm going out of state. You can count on that.

Faison

I got this toothpick habit. One of the things that Tate's wife, Marilyn, didn't especially like about me. I could always feel it, so I made it a point never to be without one in my mouth when she was around. It never bothered June Lee—my wife. Some things bother one wife. Some things bother another wife. One wife bothers the other wife. The other wife bothers the other wife. Life is hell.

I keep a box of wooden rounds—toothpicks—on my dresser and every morning load eight to twelve into my shirt pocket or somewhere. Sometimes if I'm wearing a T-shirt I'll stick them under my belt, or in a sock. If I put them in my back pocket, they break when I sit down.

Today, I drove over to Truck Freight to get Uncle Grove's footstone. It was addressed to me and Tate both. He called us, said it was coming. Said it was a secret, not to tell anybody. The shipping receipt said: Granite base 40 × 17, bronze nameplate, flower vase. Origin: Cutler, Arkansas, 72012. Pretty damn big piece of rock to be coming through the mail.

So I'm the one, not Tate, ended up running this little errand. Tate was flying his new airplane, new used airplane, and what the hell, this was something pretty straightforward, I figured, the kind of thing I do better than Tate anyway. Pick up the footstone, hold on to it until Uncle Grove dies and gets sent back to North Carolina or until just before he dies, and then put it in the graveyard, get somebody to dig the grave and all that. I always consider that I had to learn from having to be a man, from having to bear brunts. Not bragging or anything. Just the way it is. I never got any fame, war medal, college degree, degrees, all that shit. But I did live with Uncle Grove for six months when I was sixteen and Tate didn't. Hell, nobody didn't stop *him* from running off and going and staying with Uncle Grove, either. He could have done it as easy as me.

Uncle Grove's thing is, he's got this thing about being buried in the church cemetery. He's called me and Tate two or three times in the last few years to talk about it. See, everybody in the family—except me and Tate— hates him because of my mother running off and all that, way back. So if he does die or something then we got to bury him under cover. Bad blood—one of those deals. He was my mama's brother. She run off when I was seven and Tate was still at her tit. Uncle Grove didn't have anything to do with it, but the family just connects them together somehow.

So I get over to Truck Freight and ask the guy can I check it out—the thing was in a cardboard box—to be sure I got the right one. He was looking a little sleepy. The footstone was resting on a forklift about four inches off my truck bed. I pulled out my razor knife and split the cardboard. And Uncle Grove's footstone was—now listen to this—*cracked in two*. Right down the middle. Little bits of granite and granite dust resting there in the fissure. That sucker was sure as hell broke in half.

"I don't think I can use it," I said. "Not like at." Pulled me out a fresh toothpick.

"Think you can use part of it?" the guy says.

"*Part* of it?" I say. "Well, no, I don't think so. I don't see how."

"I guess not. Well . . ."

"Think insurance'll cover it?" I ask him.

"I don't see why not. What's that sticking out there?" I pushed back the cardboard. It was the brass plate, and on it was, to the left, "L. B. Grove," above his birth date—1901—and to the right "Tina," just above her birth date, 1919. Along the bottom in giant letters was "McCord," and in the middle, surrounded by these carved flowers, was "Forever Together."

"Wait a minute," I said. "There was just supposed to be one name on here, my uncle's."

Course, he don't know nothing about that. So I figure what the hell is going on? Is Aunt Tina planning to be buried out there, too? We hadn't figured out how we're going to get *him* in there, much less her, too. If everybody around here dies before he does—the old ones— then no problem. There won't be nobody around to care. But if he goes early we're going to have to drop back and punt.

"*Both* names?" says Tate, when I stop by his place. He's got this apartment. Marilyn got the house. "But the whole idea," he says, "was it was just going to be him. If he dies before Aunt Bette and Aunt Ansie we're going to play hell getting him buried out there in our section—much less her. I never bargained on this.''

"Maybe they'll outlive everybody and we can just bury them wherever we want to," I said. We've got this family section out there. "Somebody's got to start dying soon," I said.

And I hope to hell it's Ma Laura. The thing is, if me and Tate get the homeplace, I want to sell it and use my part to retire and start a little business at the same time. I got a idea for a business—called Removall, get rid of anything. Refrigerators. Garages. Anything. Rich people would love it.

I worked my ass off on that homeplace when I was growing up and I can't see it going to Faye just because she happens to be the daughter of my stepmother. Tate's got this thing about keeping it, or most of it, for a damn airport or something like that. Bullshit.

"You got any beer?" I say.

"I think there's some in there. Will insurance cover it—broken like that?" he wants to know.

"You think I can't handle this or something?" Tate's got this way.

"I'm just asking," he says. "What if he comes and wants to see where we put it?"

"We'll cross that bridge when we get to it." I was in the kitchen. I opened a can of Miller Lite. "Why don't you get some beer?" I asked him. "I figured you'd start buying real beer when Marilyn left."

"Marilyn didn't leave. I left."

Man, I was glad I didn't have to put up with Marilyn anymore. She was cold as a frozen gun barrel—didn't like the way I ate, dressed, picked my teeth, burped, other normal goddamn things. You figure it.

Adam

Pa Grove stands out in his garden almost every day. My father-in-law: Pa Grove. That's what he wants me to call him. Southern backwoods malarkey.

His garden's not much of a garden anymore. A few tomato plants is all he's had the last few years. He stands around out there in the middle of it and just looks, sometimes points to where the tomatoes or something used to be planted. Talks to himself. Marsville. And if you happen to be standing out there close enough to hear him, God forbid, he'll talk your head off.

Every summer until two or three years ago he'd have us take Polaroid pictures of him and his biggest tomatoes. We'd have to use that Polaroid. No other way. You try to use a Nikon and he'll start throwing things at you.

Same with big-mouth bass. You had to use the Polaroid.

He was using a boat until about three years ago when Bobbie got the Forest Service to present him with a certificate declaring him a nuisance to the Arkansas boating world—some kind of retirement-from-boating thing. She still takes him fishing though—sets him down on a lakeshore somewhere in a lawn chair for an afternoon.

He sent the pictures to his nephews, Faison and Tate. Tate is a college professor and Faison is a bum. They've been through here to see him several times. They'll sit and listen to his stories of wild people in his traveling shows—a man who ate the heads off rats. Of course he lets you know it was a ''nigger.'' Stories of running away from North Carolina to Arkansas, gold mining in California.

Bobbie—and I, to a lesser extent—have tried every damned way under the sun to convince him to forget about going back to North Carolina—to all that prehistory, that aboriginal, Java man, wooly mammoth prehistory, especially to be buried, for crying out loud. At least we've got a community in Arkansas—a community not all that different from Ann Arbor, for example, if you want to know the truth. It's really a very nice little university town.

We more or less humor him about going back to North Carolina to be buried. I mean all the family that's left back there, except for the boys, hate him anyway because of his sister, Evelyn, leaving her husband and sons forty years ago, and because of whatever he later did—told them off, I guess, like he's prone to do. It just wouldn't do to *really* send him back there to be buried. Bobbie wants to have him cremated in Little Rock. And she's his daughter so I try to stay out of it. But he enjoys talking about going back to North Carolina, and this little trip we'll be making in the spring is working out conveniently because it looks like we can drop him off for a week. Faison and Tate say they can take care of him and we need a vacation. Bad. He's getting to be a serious drain on us. Ma Tina is still in pretty good shape. But we're going to have to inquire soon about a home to place him in. We've got to think of ourselves, too.

The latest thing is somebody stole his and Ma Tina's gravestone. It was unreal. I cannot for the life of me understand why someone would steal someone else's gravestone. But that's what it's come to. I shouldn't be surprised. The next thing, people are going to start stealing from vegetable gardens. You watch.

Grove

When I met Anna, sweet thing, I was sixteen and she was fourteen and she was standing beside that post in the church cabin, looking up at me, and a few months later we told each other a lot of things. She said she'd be still loving me when she was old, no matter what, and I told her the same thing—and hell, it all turned out in the end that she was probably the best one of them all. And then something happened, we . . . what did happen? And then I got into trouble after the first one I married. I should have married Anna to start with. And at that church is where I got saved, accepted Jesus

Christ as my personal savior, making me forever safe from the world.

We all played games in that graveyard on Sunday nights after church and sitting on the ground out there leaning up against a tombstone is where I first kissed her—our secret place. Tombstone said "Valentine" on it. The Valentine family. That fit the bill more or less.

Me and Anna had finally said years later, one day we were sitting in the Columbia Grill—she was working for the phone company—that we'd outlast everybody and get married when we were ninety and sit together in a one-room house with doors in all the walls, so we could get out quick at the same time. That's what we said, sitting right there in the Columbia Grill.

But lord, Anna died. Yep. Years and years ago. She was buried in that same church graveyard. Where she said she would be. It's a sad thing to see somebody go like that—somebody stringing along all that secret stuff in your head. Nothing left. They just take it right with them. On out of sight. Gone.

She never left Summerlin, and her ugly husband is probably still alive and kicking and he'll probably get buried right beside her. If I get buried there, I'll sneak over. You are history longer than you are fact.

I think Tina wants to be buried in Arkansas with all her folks but just won't say it.

Hell, I can't be buried beside *all* my wives.

And that church cabin had been a place where I'd never felt anything but good, and safe, and that's long gone too, but hell, right there beside the graveyard is where it *used* to be. And now I'm ready for a narrow clay bed. I can't imagine anything better. And Doc

51

Cloverfield has give me the final word. I got it in the prostrate, and I won't allow no operating. Not down there. Not on that.

I already sent the footstone. Four-Eyes thinks somebody stole it. Tate and Faison are setting it all up for me.

I taught those boys all I could while I was there. But of course, it'll never be like it used to be, back when you got in a wagon on a Sunday afternoon, the whole family, and went to visit another family. When you, by god, had your own place to fish. People don't know the good life anymore. Fresh sausage stored in the smokehouse in soft, green corn shucks. Different families using the same smokehouse. You marked your meat and nobody bothered it. It was a different time.

Course times was tough, too. When you're on the way to my grandpa's old place, on the left side of the road around that house that was just before it, there was six rows of black-eyed peas and there was more grass in one row than there was peas in all. One Saturday, Cooper was at his ball game, see. He joined the ball team you know and played ball but I wadn't hardly living up there then as far as that goes—I was, but anyway I wadn't. Cooper, my little brother.

And I was supposed to stay there and work them peas, get the grass out of them. And Wally Womble come up there and wanted me to go with him to the company mill, the old mill place. He was going to carry some stuff down there and get it ground. So he says to Mama, "Aunt Eula, I'll come back and help him. Let him go with me to the mill," he says, "and we'll come back and work the peas."

She said all right, but you know when we left the millpond and headed back? Right close to sundown.

And she whipped me something terrible. See, you can see it. See? Look here. See those scars? I was bull-headed enough then to stick up both hands like this, and I says, Help yourself. And she really put it on me. She took the blood out of me. Oh, boy.

Now I stand out here amongst these dried-up tomato vines. Maybe there's a little green knot-head tomato still down here somewhere that I can wrap up in newspaper and stick in the closet.

Nope. There ain't.

Now what is it, I wonder, that would set the world up like it's been set up? Would it be God that would set the world up, set me up in it, set up a mama and papa and brothers and sisters and friends and a place to live and fields and pretty spring days and good food and cold snow and a fireplace and ponds and creeks, and then jerk it all right out from under me by killing off my old man when I was a boy, for no reason in the world, except that diseases had been allowed, diseases that wiped out men and women in their strongest days, whether or not they had any children, or had just a few, or a whole lot?

Mama shouldn't never have whipped me like that, because I felt like why should I have to stay there and get the grass out of them peas when Cooper was gone to play ball.

And Evelyn, lord have mercy, was she a dandy? My sister. She'd hook that little old crooked-legged mule up to the wagon and go down and cut a load of wood like a man. Could ride a horse, bareback, like nothing you ever seen. Shoot a gun. Had her own rabbit gums. That's right.

I've forgotten what that little old crooked-legged mule's name was.

She got whipped, too. For all the normal things. She got where she'd sit around behind the store and smoke cigarettes. That store had been there since way before cars, and there was a hitching post out in front of it. So . . . see, girls didn't smoke back then, nowhere, but she was going out behind the store and smoking with the storeowner's daughter, who was mean. Somebody told Papa, and he made her stand at the hitching post and smoke five cigarettes in a row for five days in a row. Every day the crowd got a little bigger and a little bigger. She stopped smoking, too.

I imagine of all the people in the family, me and her was the closest. She'd go hunting with me, and we had fights. She never forgot some of the things that happened. One time I held up a rabbit from one of my gums to show her, cause she didn't get any that morning, and that rabbit jerked loose and went running off and she fell on the ground laughing. She told about that over and over. She could actually skin a rabbit faster than I could. That's no lie. She was quicker than me in some ways, once she growed up a little bit. I'm talking about when she was around thirteen, fourteen, and I was eighteen or nineteen, before I stopped living up there and then run off after Mama married old man Harper.

Aw, there's a lot of different things that I could tell, you know, about the whole entire country around in there and everywhere from Bethel all the way back to the old mill place and down below up the old ah, ah penitentiary place and all the way coming back into Summerlin, where we used to go and what we used to do, but it's hard to remember a lot of that stuff. And, that was before World War I.

And now here I am with my groin getting eat out. Looks like I would be allowed to go out peaceable. They say He works in mysterious ways. Well, I do too.

Faison

Tate keeps his place pretty nice. I been aiming to put up some kind of blinds, shades, in mine, something on my windows. What's hanging in my bedroom is a poncho, and when I got back from Tate's, I looked through the head hole to see if I could see that dog out back that had been barking for the last two days solid. But there's a row of bushes at the back end of the yard that hides him.

At least I never had this problem living at the motel. Didn't have to worry about no curtains either.

I headed for the kitchen, got a beer.

I was thinking.

Few minutes later, I stood on their porch and knocked on their screen door. I saw them moving in a couple of weeks ago.

One window on each side of the front door. The window shades were pulled down—gold colored. A TV was on somewhere in there. I opened the screen door and knocked. The door come open on its own.

I stuck my head in. TV noises from in there in that first room on the left. Fishing gear was on the floor of a hall that ran front to back. I closed the door behind me, tried to see what make the fishing reels were—one was a Penn. I knocked on the door to the room.

This voice from inside: "Yeah?"

"I need to talk to somebody."

"Just a minute." The door opened. Short, stocky man, reddish hair, scrawny mustache—little clusters of red hairs like. "What do you want?" he says.

"I got a complaint. That dog out back's about to drive me crazy. He's been barking for—"

"It's my brother's, but he's asleep. He'll be leaving in a week or so, and he'll take the dog with him. So you don't have nothing to worry about."

The guy was acting like, hey, no big deal. But for *me* it *was*. So I said, "Well, you go wake him up, because something's got to give here. That dog's driving me crazy." He had already started shutting the door.

"Hey," he said, opening the door again. "He's got a nerve problem. I can't bother him right now."

"Can't *bother*—"

"You live around here?" He looked over his shoulder at the TV.

"Yeah. I live right out there."

"Well, he's asleep now, and I ain't waking him up. He's pretty nervous."

"Look, man, either somebody shuts up the dog, or I

shut up the dog. I don't have to sit in my own house and be disturbed by some dog after I give a warning. This is a warning. Okay? I mean this has been going on two whole days and nights. It's driving me crazy.''

This is the kind of situation where Uncle Grove would kick ass. I been with him when he did.

"Give me your phone number," he says. He could see I was serious. He writes down my phone number on a newspaper.

"If I ain't heard from him by five o'clock," I say, "I'll figure nothing ain't going to be done."

"I'll give him the number," he says. "He'll call."

So I come on back home and I'm thinking: I go out and talk to this guy. Right? He acts like I'm the one bothering *him*. He's mouthing off at *me*. Now ain't this something? This is the guy with the barking dog. And who's mouthing off at who? There's people like this all over the world. They don't think about nothing but theirselves. They're everywhere, and when you bring it to their attention, they go all to pieces. And a bigger problem is the people that let them get by with it. You got jerks all over the place that won't say nothing to these kind of assholes. They'd rather get run all over. They'd rather avoid a little trouble. They're what's wrong with this country.

I got my twelve-gauge Remington automatic out of the closet, found a box of shells, buckshot, in the top dresser drawer, got out seven, dropped them on the bed. By god, if I did end up shooting this dog, the dog wouldn't just be dead. He'd be dead dead. I wouldn't do nothing like this half-ass.

The Remington is my daddy's. Was my daddy's. He

probably didn't use it no more than eight or ten times in his life. He gave it to me after he got sick this last time. Last long time. He took me quail hunting a few times when I was little, but hell, I did more stuff like that with Uncle Grove in the six months I stayed with him than I did with my daddy all my life. Hunting, fishing, stuff like that.

Uncle Grove used to have a bunch of guns. He's still got that one that was handed down—the double-barrel with the old-fashioned hammers, handed down from his daddy, my mama's daddy—the gun that was in a fight at a liquor still, got hit with buckshot. Uncle Grove told me that story a bunch of times. His daddy had to pick buckshot out of this nigger's head. Black man.

Mama told me some stuff, too. I remember her letting me sew one time—stick a needle with a white thread through a button hole. And I remember her chasing me around the house one time, and driving me to town in a car. She was pretty.

Phone rang. "Hello." It was the guy with the dog. Okay, I thought, let's see what's coming down here.

"You the one wanted me to call you?"

"Yeah. That dog has been barking for two solid days and nights, and it's driving me crazy."

"I think I can get him quiet," he says.

"That's good," I said. "You want to take him in the house, fine. It ain't my problem. But if I have to, I'll—"

"Where you located?"

"Out your back door and to the left. That's my house." No way to meet this kind of thing but head-on, so I said, "I'll meet you out at the bushes there if you want to."

So I go on out there and when I *see* this guy, I say, "You're the same guy!"

"Nah," he says. "He's my twin brother."

"You ain't the same one?" They looked exactly alike.

"No way. Now look here," he says, "the dog was just barking, that's all."

"I know he was just barking. That's what he's been doing for two days and nights. That's the problem."

The dog starts yelping. Right then and there. So the guy acts a little nervous.

I yell, "Shut up!"

The dog stops barking. The guy looks at me, at the dog. "Good boy," he says to the dog.

There was a break in the bushes—a path. "Let me see the dog," I said. "I know something about dogs." I do, too. I walked on through.

The dog was in one side of a double garage. A motorboat was in the other side, where the sun shined in, propped up on a little refrigerator. The dog was standing in the shady part, breathing vapor, chain running from his collar through a hole in the back of the garage and all these cages the size of suitcases laying around in there.

Dog wagged his tail, pranced on his front paws. I put out my fist. The dog licked it. "It's a Doberman," I said, squatting down. "Or mostly Doberman."

Another dog, a pointer—liver and white—stood up from behind the boat. He stretched and shook off all over. "Whose pointer?" I said. "He's right pretty."

"Jimmy's. I bought them both, gave Jimmy the bird dog. He *is* pretty."

"Looks like a bird dog I used to have. I was going to give my boy a bird dog."

"What happened?"

"He died," I said.

"I had a pit bull die on me three, four years ago. But he'd been eat up pretty good before I bought him."

"My boy died," I said.

"Damn. I'm sorry. What happened? Or . . . you know."

"Car wreck." I didn't want to get into all that. "You hunt any?"

"Used to. But I quit shooting the birds. What's your name?"

"Faison."

"I quit shooting the birds, Faison. You know, got tired of it. But Jimmy still hunts. Goes all the time."

Right here I thought, man. Here's a bird dog—good-looking bird dog. Here's somebody at my back door that likes to hunt birds. I hadn't been hunting in a long, long time. "What are all those cages for?" I couldn't figure that one out.

"Snakes. Jimmy's a snake handler. Does shows for schools and stuff."

"Has he got any in there? Maybe that's why—"

"Naw, he's out of snakes right now. He lets them out under the neighbors' houses."

"What? He *what*?"

"Just kidding. He sells them, lets them out in the woods, different stuff. He's supposed to be getting some new ones. Jimmy don't stay out of snakes long." He patted the bird dog's head, looked at me. "He says he's going bird hunting in the morning. Try out that dog. Dog's been broke. Think you might want to go?"

"Well. Yeah, I'll go bird hunting. I'll go bird hunting."

The pointer had good blood. You could tell. A beautiful dog. "But we got to do something about this other one's barking." I said.

"We'll work something out. We'll bring him inside if he keeps it up. His name is Cactus. Hey, *Jimmy*," he yelled.

Jimmy came to the back door. They *were* twins.

"What's up?" says Jimmy.

"This guy—what's your name again?"

"Faison."

"Faison wants to go hunting with you in the morning. He's a old bird hunter."

"Sure. Come on out about six-thirty. I need somebody to go with me. Timmy won't go. He got saved or something. Something happened."

"I just decided to stop shooting the birds. That's all."

"I'll be here," I said. "I hope he's a good dog."

"He's a good dog. He better be."

Then they took the Doberman inside.

That was about as simple as you could ask for. Stand your ground, don't blink, nine times out of ten things will work out for you.

June Lee

Since me and Faison broke up I've moved twice, but the place I got now, I like best. It's an apartment in the basement of a nice two-story home in Cherry Hill Acres. I got my own entrance, kitchen, parking place. And out back is a little patch of woods that's real nice. I've been walking out there some.

It seems like me and Faison can't get around to a divorce. Everybody else I know, *everybody*, has been divorced. Faison's brother, too. I liked his wife all right. We ate over there some. She got the house. Their boy is weird, and I think that kind of comes from her, actually.

Faison or me don't really want a divorce, so we keep seeing each other—here and there, one way or another. Since Junior died, it's been hard. That car wreck was the event of my life, and I did some counseling with Preacher Gordon, but it got to be the same kind of thing over and over, the counseling. I do think he helped me in some ways. But some things you just can't change.

To let you know about how we are together—me and Faison—it's almost like the last fight we had. It's almost like that explains it.

We were out in the backyard in broad daylight. "It was a promise!" he yelled. Screaming. "You promised to change his name. It was a goddamned promise!" He just kept yelling this over and over, about the *name*. Like Junior was *his*, and like that dumb name change was more important than anything else. He was acting crazy.

I slapped him, I had to, and screamed right back at him, "He was mine, you son of a bitch. You don't have no rights in any of this."

He grabbed me by the arm and pulled me toward the garage. I tried to get away. He was acting crazier than I'd ever seen him.

He got me in the tool room—off the garage—and while I was scrambling to get back out I grabbed a shelf beside the door and it pulled down and stuff started falling all around us and I felt him ease up, soften up, come to his senses and right there I realized with some kind of jolt that I was there in that tool room with the only person in the world I had. The only one. And in that minute that everything was falling down in the tool shed, I just reached down and put my hand on Faison, you know, like I used to do when we were playing around. We always played around a lot. And he melted. Right there in the tool room. Then he won't melted, if you know what I mean. And for a minute I turned loose all he'd done with the lies when we got married. See, Faison was all I had in the world, except God. That's one of the things I couldn't straighten out with Preacher Gordon. If God reasons out things that happen, like they say at church, He didn't have no reason to let that happen to us, Junior getting killed in a car wreck, with me driving. No God could ever have a reason for letting that happen.

Faison showed up this afternoon.

"I brought you some mail," he said, standing in the

door. Then he just started right in talking, came on in like he lives here, you know.

"You been drinking?" I asked him. I could smell it.

"Couple of beers," he said.

He started telling me about his Uncle Grove's footstone getting cracked in two when it was being shipped.

"Cracked in two?" I said.

"That's right. Cracked in two right down the middle. There was this brass plate won't harmed none, but that stone, man, was sure cracked in two."

"Why was he shipping a footstone?" I asked him. At that moment, Faison *had* to be thinking about Junior's footstone, too. He couldn't be standing there talking about a footstone and not be thinking about Junior's.

"He wants me and Tate to set him up a place to be buried. That's all I know. So I guess we will." Then he sat on the sofa, kind of looked around, casual-like. "Listen to this," he says. "There was this dog barking out back yesterday. Been barking for days. So I go out there and this guy acts like I'm the one with the problem. You know, your typical—"

"You want a Coke?" I knew he was getting into a long-winded story about something.

"Got a beer?" he says. He knows I don't have no beer.

"You know I don't have no beer, Faison."

"Just give me some water, then. So," he says, "this guy acts like I'm the one with the problem. This is the way people are all over the place. You point out a problem and it's *you* got the problem. You know what I mean?"

64

I told him I did. I do, too—because I know Faison Bales.

"But it turned out good," he says.

I handed him a glass of water. Just like him, he hadn't said nothing about my place. Real nice little kitchen area. Just perfect, you know, for one person.

"So anyway," he says, "this turns out to be a pretty decent guy after all, and hell, I end up getting a chance to go hunting. Tomorrow probably. With the one I didn't think I liked. They were twins—Jimmy and Timmy. We're going fishing sometime, too, probably."

"You're going to get killed hunting and drinking, Faison. It's stupid." He is very stupid that way.

"You know," he says—he throws his arm up on the couch, getting really settled in—"I ain't been hunting since before, you know, Junior died."

Something snapped. "Faison . . ." I didn't want to hear any more. Nothing.

"What?" he says. Real surprised-like. This stuff builds up in me when he's away.

"Faison," I said, "will you please put that tombstone back? It's been over a year, and legally, it's against the law to have that footstone out there with the wrong name on it. I ain't going to just forget it. You know I'm going to do something about it if you don't."

"June Lee, let's don't get started on that."

"You know I'll switch it back if you don't, Faison."

"Shit, June Lee, you know I'll switch it back if you switch it back."

"You lied to me, Faison." He told me he'd never been married, never really loved anybody, all this.

65

"June Lee," he says, "if I'd had the slightest idea it meant all that much to you, I'd a told you before I did."

"You lie. You knew it would of made a difference and that's why you lied in the first place."

"I didn't lie in the first place."

"Come off it, Faison."

"I think we ought to forget it. The footstone's in place and that was our agreement, June Lee. We made an agreement."

"I ain't talking about the footstone, Faison."

"Listen, June Lee, I want to ask you something," he says. Going into his serious Mr. Lawyer mode. "Okay," he says. "I just thought about this the other night. What if you *had* known I'd been married? What then?"

Faison has this way of letting his face go into these expressions that may or may not go along with what he's saying. And he'll find a spot over your shoulder and stare at that instead of look you in the eye.

"It was more than if I'd known you'd been married, Faison. You know that. But if I had known just that," I said, "then I'd known I was marrying a honest man."

I've had a hard time with men in my life.

"Honest, huh? I don't understand why it's so damned important about this stuff that's history. Sure, I was married. But it was a failure. I put it behind me. It was a failure. Like they say, you buy what you pay for."

"You buy what you . . . ? Faison. And I don't know why," I said, "it's so important for you to have a boy that won't yours in the first place named after you. That's history too, Faison."

He stood up. "I got to get out of here," he says.

"Good. Good. You just walk away from it, Faison. You always were good at that. Walking away. You'll be walking away when you die."

That got his attention. He slammed the storm door so hard, the glass broke.

I yelled, "Which won't be one minute too soon!"

Thank god the Pattersons—upstairs—were gone. The glass fell on the outside, not the inside. Several big pieces. One leaned against the door. I just stood there—started biting a fingernail. I've been trying real hard to stop doing that.

Why couldn't Faison have been just a little bit more like Tate, and had some ambition, some sense about moving up in the world? If he'd been different then there wouldn't have been a fight that day, the day I started out in the car. Why couldn't he have just been a little bit different?

Can't live with him, can't live without him. Damned if I do. Damned if I don't.

At some point I'm going to have to change that footstone back myself. I know where I can find some help.

4

Gloria

*I*TS LIKE MR. GLENN MORE OR LESS GIVE UP. I HAVE
to prop his back up with the pillows, then get his legs
down off the side of the bed for circulation. He's lasted
a long time this way, and Miss Laura she going down
so fast, I think maybe he be the one to outlast her,
instead of the other way round.

Miss Laura, she can stand on the floor and walk over
to the window and back. We still do that twice a day.
Once at ten and once at three. Social services all for
that. But sometime it seem like she don't even know
where she is. She don't even look out the window no
more like she used to. She used to would stop and stand
there a little while and mumble a little something. Now

when she get over there she just turn around and head back like she be glad to lay back down.

She used to mostly talk about Mr. Glenn, about all she had to do for him for all that time before she got sick. She tell me about having to pick him up outen the bathroom floor and all that. She tell about other stuff over and over, too. That's where he kept falling—in the bathroom. But at least she had one of them high commode tops, which I didn't know nothing about while Lorenzo were down and out. You get a little bitty low commode down close to the floor, and you try to get a sick man, a dying sick man, down and then up off it without him toppling over in the floor, then you be doing a pretty good balancing act. You be leaning back with all your weight pulling him up and if your hand slip loose you go over backwards yourself. And once he topple down there on the way down, instead of on the way up, then you know where he gone shit. He gone shit in the floor. And who gone clean it up? Mr. Clean? Michael Jordan?

How bout them naming that highway after Michael Jordan? Pick my chicken. What that young whippersnapper done to get a road named after him except look out after hisself, doing what he love to do all his short life, big and strong with all that natural gift from God? What else he done? Seem like to me the one they name the road after would be somebody who done looked after somebody they *have* to look after—while they love the person but hate all that cleaning up and toting and heaving and lifting and shaving and wiping and feeding and scraping dried-up stuff you don't know what it is off the floor and the table legs. Humph. And you doing all this when you ain't feeling so good yourself and ain't got enough money to buy no bed sheets and run plum out of energy but have to keep going anyway, no matter what.

Michael Jordan? You think he ever short on bed sheets? And if he ever been, you think he ain't more than made up for it? And they name the road after Michael Jordan?

I know Miss Laura she done a lot, because Lorenzo he only lasted bout two and a half years after he got down. Mr. Glenn he lasted I think about eleven years. And them boys of his not much help. Course my chiren was the same way.

When I was growing up people took care of the old folks. We did, anyway.

What would get me down most is Lorenzo's bowels, you know. And then there's no worse smell in bed sheets than piss less it be bedsores. Lord a mercy I would *keep* sheets in the tub. I wish I'd had the washamachine that's here at Mr. Glenn's. If anybody wanted to know what I needed I'd say lord honey I could sure use a washamachine.

What about my little hallway with the cracks in the floor I travel back and forth on to the bathroom with my Lorenzo. Why don't the government pave that and name that after Michael Jordan? Sha. I just don't get it. A man make his living jumping up and down with people screaming all over the place and him making enough money to pave Hanson County three times over in gold-plated concrete getting a big four-lane highway named after him while at the same time hundreds of little women in North Carolina breaking their own backs scrubbing up after a sick, broke-down husband who done worried hisself down to a nub after sixty-five years of toting shingles and nailing roofs and these little women can't buy a pair of bed sheets cause they cost so much—you looked at the price of bed sheets lately?—and they don't have time to powder their nose much less wipe their *own* ass and they don't even get *their* names wrote down in a . . . a two-bit beggarman's matchbook.

The world is a funny place.

The problem is that people don't have the eyes and hearts to judge up on somebody like me or Miss Laura, but they shore judge up Mr. Basketball.

Law, I don't usually get riled up but sometimes I do. My son Lorenzo Junior's the one crazy about that Michael Jordan. We call him Lorenzo now, we used to call him Junior. He drove to Wilmington to pier-fish, told me about that road, that new I-40 they made such a fuss over.

Oh yeah, speaking of Junior, Mr. Bullock, he name his two twin sons the same as him—William Dean, Jr., and William Dean, Jr. So, somebody say, what you call them? and he say, Billy Dean and Billy Dean, and somebody say, really, is that so? well, how you tell them apart? and he say, oh, one's a little darker than the othern.

Speaking of chiren, that teenager that spends the night over here brought her little boy the other night. She's got two I think. I didn't say nothing, but I don't think Faye would like that. She don't do a very good job, but it's hard to find somebody that do. I don't know what they pay her. She ain't much older than that boy of

71

Tate's and got two boys herself. There ought to be a law against marrying before you're growed up.

Tate brought that boy of his over here for a visit this afternoon. Mr. Glenn always asking after him. And he always saying stuff to Tate like, "You been by to see Bette lately? You seen Ansie lately? You took Morgan by to see them lately? Bring him by to see me again real soon, Son," and you can tell by the way that boy of Tate's walk that he ain't interested in setting the first foot on the first porch step to this here place.

He follow his daddy on in there, lagging behind, and Mr. Glenn see him and kind of light up and put out his hand, and I wonder can he see all that hair and all them clothes with the holes in the knees, and that earring, and soldier boots, and stuff like that. Nobody in my family ever wore the first piece of clothing with the first hole in it or the first patch that show. I don't understand what get into their heads. What could make a child like that?

Morgan

On the way to the airfield, Dad decided to stop by and see Granddad and then Aunt Bette and Aunt Ansie. It's like all these generations or something. He didn't say anything about going to see them until we got in the car and I didn't have a choice. I'm glad Mom doesn't have a bunch of relatives to visit. Especially old ones. It would be okay if there was something to do once we get there. But it's the same old stuff over and over. And then they beg me to come back—which would be okay with me if it was like *interesting*.

About the time we passed Uncle Sam's Army Surplus, I thought about the stuff we'd been studying in history and all that stuff Mom told me about Dad's medal, so I asked Dad, "How many people did you know that got killed in the war?"

"Right many," he says. He glanced over at me.

"What about the time you like won the medal?"

"I had a good friend who got shot down and I tried to save him but I couldn't find him on the ground. Some clouds came in and I couldn't see him. I could talk to him on the radio, but that's it."

"Radio?"

"He had a hand-held radio and was trying to tell me where he was. Why are you suddenly interested in this?"

I told him we had some stuff going on in school about it. Actually I was wondering if he'd tell me the same story he told Mom that "broke her heart."

We drove awhile. Then I said, "Is that the story that broke Mom's heart?"

"That's part of it."

So I was like waiting.

He says, "I'll tell you all that when you're a little older. There's some stuff I'm kind of ashamed of, and it's all complicated somehow."

So I wondered what could it be that I couldn't understand now? "What happened to him?"

"I actually, ah, heard them shooting him. Over his radio."

"You did?"

"Yeah."

"Don't you think people kind of got what they deserved over there? I mean the ethical dimensions of that war were pretty awesome."

Dad braked the car—whoa, I'd gotten his attention. He slowed down, pulled over to the shoulder of the road, and looked at me.

"Naw, Son," he says, "I don't think he got what he deserved. He was my best friend," he says.

"This is my teacher's idea," I said. "Don't look at me."

Next, it's visit Granddad, then the aunts, and then if I'm good, he'll take me flying in this like slow and low antique airplane.

What he can't get through his head is this: I'm into computers. He does not see how the knowledge of operating a computer, creating applications, is like real knowledge. I think he still sees it as reading directions—what everybody who hates computers thinks. They don't see computers as tools to do jobs. The only way Dad will use a computer is as a word processor. He gets somebody else to do all the analysis. Surveys and things where he's gone into such and such a business place and asked questions. He used to talk about it at home, and then he talked less and less about it. Mom tells her friends about how he talked less and less.

I can remember when I was about ten and they'd talk

to each other a lot. Her business is interior design. And then they got to talking less and less and yelling more and more. Awesome arguments. Then they wouldn't speak to each other for two or three days, and they'd be real jumpy all the time. And then they'd argue about me, what I was supposed to watch on TV, what I was supposed to eat, what I was supposed to wear. And what I wanted was like a brother or sister.

I got into computers and music early and Mom would support me in all kinds of ways. And Dad had this thing about guns and farms. He gave me that gun when I was *thirteen*. I didn't want a gun. I wanted a Hayes-compatible modem.

I tried to say, okay, look, here are the kinds of things you can accomplish with a modem. This is what a modem is for. I tried to explain to him about bulletin boards creating a world community—global network and such as that. You can get all kinds of stuff out of an information bank, with detail you wouldn't *believe*. And what you can do with music is awesome. You can play it and the computer writes it. You can write it and the computer plays it.

At Granddad's place we went on in like we usually do. It's what used to be a farm. I did what I usually do, which is go in and stand by the bed and watch Granddad cry a little and talk some. We don't go in to see my step-grandmother because of some kind of family feud or something. It's pretty boring.

This whole scene is something Mom and Dad used to argue about—about inheritance, who gets the farm, which is worth over a million dollars, and all that.

Before we left Granddad's to go over to Aunt Bette's,

we walked across the field behind the house, and back. Dad's got this idea about landing his airplane out there. And he always shows me the foundation of this house where he and Uncle Faison grew up.

At Granddad's the outside is still pretty neat, and inside everybody is dying, but at Aunt Bette's it's like the outside is kind of dying, and inside everybody's fine. This lawnmower and old wringer washing machine sit out there in her garage. My cousin, Junior, took that lawnmower apart and put it back together before he was killed in a car wreck. I don't like agree that he should have died in the car wreck, but he could be a real pain in the ass when he wanted to. Mom said he inherited backwardness. But she said that before he got killed.

We stepped onto the back porch and I saw through the glass panes in the door that Aunt Ansie was visiting Aunt Bette. They live close together. They were sitting at the kitchen table.

Aunt Bette looked up when Dad tapped on the door and opened it.

"Well, hey, son," she says to Dad. "Have a seat." Then she sees me and goes bananas, exclaiming this, that, and the other, reaching her arms out to me, skin like vacuum-cleaner bags hanging from between her elbows and armpits.

"Good gracious," said Aunt Ansie. "Me too."

So I, you know, hug her, too. Dad catches me rolling my eyes.

Bette

It's clear that Tate was the one turned out best, except for his divorce. Faison is a outright failure. No job to speak of. He's been divorced too, and is, as far as I can tell, separated now. That's what they say, anyway. I don't try to keep up anymore.

"Well, Lord help my time," I said to the boy, "look who's here. Hey, sonny boy, give your Aunt Bette a hug." He ain't exactly warm toward people, which is one of his problems. You can look at him and tell he's got more problems than that. He's grown two feet since I seen him last.

I pulled out a couple of chairs and asked them if they didn't want a piece of pie. I thought to myself, What has brought this youngin out and about? I didn't want to talk about him to his face. He seems . . . well, he seems . . . kind of queer. Some of Evelyn's blood? Me and Ansie have talked about it. But all that was a secret, so we decided long ago never to mention it except to ourselves and maybe to somebody if in the end we end up with absolutely none of the homeplace, which it is looking more and more like we might do. We worked that place sixty-odd year between us and for us to end up in the poorhouse while that Faye, or Faison, especially, gets half of it and sells it for no telling what in this day and age—to have all that happen is a outright wrong.

"Just a small piece for me," said Tate. Talking about

the pie. "I might could force it down." That's what he always says. At least he does come by once in a while.

"Been flying that airplane?" I asked him. Why in the world he'd want to buy a airplane is beyond me. He ought to know they're dropping like flies all over the place.

"Oh yeah, we're on the way out to the airfield now."

"Here you go," I said. I put two pieces of pie on the table. "The crust didn't turn out just right, but it's still hot," I said. "You like that airplane, son?" I asked Morgan.

He says, "Yeah."

If the government hadn't started that integration, that boy might have been taught to say "Yes ma'am." And if people hadn't started landing on the moon it might be a good world now. When they started messing with the moon, and people's habits and manners and likes and *personal* dislikes and *personal* preferences, and started mixing the races, they went too far.

"So how's your daddy getting along?" I asked Tate.

"I think he's doing about the same," he says. "We just dropped by to see him a little while ago."

"I was just telling Ansie," I says, "that yesterday Glenn didn't look much better to me. Any better. I wish I could get over there more. But if I take on more than I can handle, I pay for it."

"I don't think Gloria does what all she could," says Ansie. "For one thing, she don't keep water in there. She ought to keep water by the bed where he can get at it. And she ought to be making him walk. She makes Laura walk twice a day."

"Laura could have done more for him than she did

before she got sick if she'd been a mind to," I said. "Glenn ain't the reason she's sick, I don't care what Faye says."

"What's *she* said lately?" Tate wanted to know.

"She said it to Wilma and Harold," I said. So I told him. "What she said was that if her mama hadn't spent all that time waiting on Glenn, she wouldn't have ever got in the fix she's in."

That Faye has never set foot in this house, except that one time she came in the front door and sat in the living room for a few minutes—didn't even know to come in the back door—and explained all about getting somebody to set with them and the expenses and what Tate and Faison was going to pay and what *she* was going to pay and how she had it all written down and would be happy to listen to any suggestions that anybody had. And all this.

After years of Glenn going downhill and downhill, and then her insisting on him seeing that doctor from the university after he'd been seeing Dr. Umstead since he was thirty-two year old and Dr. Umstead would of never done anything but what was right and had made house visits right on up through the time that no other doctor would think of such a thing. That Faye was behind the doctor change. Miss Laura had a lot of faults, lord knows, but changing doctors wouldn't have been one of them if it hadn't been for that Faye—not even having the sense to come in the back door, into the kitchen like everybody else since the dawn of time. She had to walk all the way around the house to get to the front door. Nothing worse than somebody with no house sense.

I was hoping against hope—couldn't help but hope, and I wouldn't tell this to anybody—that Tate might say something about sharing that land with me and Ansie if it turned out that Laura died first and didn't get the whole kit and caboodle. What a *tragedy* that would be—Glenn dying first, and the land handed right down to that Faye as soon as Laura died, to be sold to some chemical plant probably for no telling how many million dollars. It's located right there at TechComm Commons, and all that land selling around there to Yankees and Japs and Arabs and anybody else with loads of crooked money taking a notion to buy.

"And you know," I said to Tate, "they'll bury Laura in the graveyard, on our plot. That's what she wants."

"Why wouldn't she be buried there?" asked the *boy*. Like this was some of his business. Like he was grown or something, which they don't tell them any better in the schools nowadays.

Ansie looked at him, Morgan, with a look that said, and *should* have said, Whose blood do you have—had *better* have—in your veins, son? Whose blood has been coursing through your body down from your grandmama and granddaddy and his daddy and on back keeping us right and true Bales with God on our side, and though we was always poor we never wanted for food and shelter and never once took nothing from nobody as help—and wouldn't have for anything in the world—and would have fought to the death to keep from taking something given to us, and loved each other seven or eight times over and you ask why shouldn't *she* be buried there?

"Son," I said, "she was from Hoke County.

"And Lord," I said to Tate—hoping to soften things up a little bit; I was taking his pie plate over to the sink—"have we seen it all? Raising you-all, taking you to the fields, pulling you in a wagon, toting you around the yard. And she come along, Laura, you know, after most of that was over. You was, what—five? And Faison, twelve? Course Faison wouldn't ever pay no attention much to us—caught between us and his real mama the way he was, I suppose."

I've said all this to both those boys many a time—I try not to play favorites though anybody can see they ain't either one been good to their daddy.

And sometimes I think about all the discipline me and Ansie had to instill because of them being tainted. We had to undress Tate and teach him about his privates. Yessir. Somebody had to teach him such. Glenn wouldn't. We was the same as their mamas. Faison got a little too old for that and had been more or less ruined anyway, by his mama, we figured. If their natural *mother* would do what she done, then it was no telling what *they* would do. We had to be careful about seeing that they knew right from wrong—especially the little one, Tate, the one we could get our hands on.

Mama told us that getting the Devil's blood out of them boys would not be easy, if possible at all. And Harold Fuller has told somebody that Grove McCord is planning on coming back. But Grove McCord has got to have more sense than that. I think he's wanted. For a crime.

It's just a shame that they had a no-count mama—and uncle. Grove could have been some help if he'd been a mind to. If he'd had a mind to do honest work—and the decency.

Me and Ansie did the best we could under the circumstances and of course it turned out with us never having any children of our own, so Tate and Faison is really all we have and it's such a shame that that boy of Tate's has turned out the way he has. Not a scant of personality and all that hair.

Tate

Morgan's eyes rolled ever so slightly as he went through the motions of hugging Aunt Bette and Aunt Ansie, one at a time. Then when they put a piece of pie in front of him, he didn't have the manners to say thank you. I had to force him to say it. He's thick. I hate to say that, and I love him, but he is.

Aunt Bette's kitchen smelled like snuff, gas heat, oilcloth, and apple pie. That close-smelling kitchen is something out of my father's life, probably my mother's life, my aunts' lives for sure, and on back until long long ago, and now forever gone out of my life except when I'm here in this kitchen, or in Aunt Ansie's kitchen. Marilyn had us a big fancy kitchen with no table in it. She had a "work station." Marilyn's kitchen was the first one in the family without a table since before Jesus.

"How y'all been?" I asked.

"Fine," said Aunt Ansie. " 'Cepin we wrecked a grocery cart yesterday."

"Wrecked a grocery cart?"

"Coming out of Food Lion."

She went into one of her long, involved stories about how they'd bought this great big cantaloupe and she was putting it in the car trunk and it dropped out of the bag and started rolling down the parking lot toward Aunt Bette, who had her back turned, pushing the cart down to one of those cart stalls. Aunt Ansie yelled, Aunt Bette turned around, put her feet together to catch it, turned loose the grocery cart, which started rolling down the hill, and on and on. The grocery cart hit a car and Aunt Bette caught the cantaloupe.

"We didn't need that cantaloupe," said Aunt Bette.

"It didn't hurt to get it. It was so pretty."

"It's a sin to waste. Carl Oakley's about to have a whole batch, for nothing."

"It's a sin to be stubborn, too."

"Where does it say that?"

"It's in there."

This is the way they go back and forth. Every now and then it gets nasty.

"How's Faison getting along?" Aunt Bette asks me. "Wait a minute. What you been up to, son?" she asks Morgan. "I ain't seen you in I don't know how long. What you been up to?"

"Nothing much."

"Well, well. I'm glad you came by to see Aunt Bette.

Aunt Bette gets lonesome staying here all alone, not able to get out so much anymore. Now, don't you wait so long before you come see me again, you hear?"

"Yeah, okay," he says. Mr. Personality.

Out at the airfield I tried to show him several things about the airplane. I opened the cowling, checked the oil, and was explaining about the exhaust system when I realized he'd just walked off and sat down on the grass.

So, hell, I went on over, sat down. "You're not too interested in all this, are you?" I said.

He tightened his bootstrings—combat boots, very practical—then mumbled, "Not especially." You'd think I was torturing him. What am I supposed to do?

"That's okay," I said. As calm as I could. "But do you think you want to go up for a ride?"

"I guess so."

I swear, I try to understand it. If my old man had bought an airplane—like Uncle Grove's—I'd have been beside myself. It would have been the best thing that ever happened. But Morgan? He sits on his butt and mopes.

I remember three or four rides with Uncle Grove when I was little—before he left. He'd put me in the front seat. He'd sit in the backseat and look over my shoulder and say, "Left hand on the throttle, right hand on the stick, feet on the rudder pedals." And I'd get all set, except my legs wouldn't reach the rudder pedals, and then he'd say, "Crank her up." And I'd turn the key, press the button—the Super Cruiser was the first airplane with an electric starter. The propeller would flip over, stop, flip over, stop, flip, catch, and come to life. I'd feel the throttle under my hand move forward—him in the backseat, working the dual controls. "Okay, push it on up," he'd say. "Push the throttle on up and stay on the controls with me. Feel what I'm doing," and we'd go bumping along the ground, with him talking loud, saying what he was doing with the rudder pedals and the throttle to get the tail end to swing one way or the other, talking about touching a brake with his heel to make her turn, checking out the controls. Moving them all around. I'd be staring straight ahead at the instrument panel, left or right out the windows. Then he'd brake her to a stop, letting up on the brakes an instant before she stopped to make the stop smooth—like stopping a boat in water, against nothing. We'd be out there at that devil's stomping ground—the worn circle in the grass between the other two circles that were growing grass back. He'd wear one circle down, then lengthen or shorten the cable.

He'd say, "Pull up that hand brake. Pull it hard. Hard. Attaboy. Don't touch the throttle now." And he'd open the door and climb out, hook up the cable, that airplane going *a-cup, a-cup, a-cup, a-cup*; then he'd get back in.

The little airplane felt like a hollow shell with a heavy engine up front, bouncing over the ground in that big wide circle, the engine wide open, picking up speed. Then clear, clear of the ground. Above the ground, broken away. A smoothness. Then in a minute we'd be free, broken away from the cable. Then my eyes on a cow down there, standing in a green pasture, not even looking up, and the whole wide world spread out below, with white wisps of clouds way, way up there above us.

"You want to follow me through on the controls?" I ask Morgan.

"Naw, I don't think so," he says.

Maybe I should be happy he's talking at all.

It seemed like he was born and then about three months later he was sixteen years old and silent.

We flew over the homeplace and I decided to go ahead and land on the cart path across the back field. The wind was just right—ten knots off the nose. We set her down and stopped with eight hundred feet to spare.

5

Jimmy

ME AND THIS GUY THAT CAME OVER ABOUT THE
dog ended up going hunting together. He really wanted
to go. Faison's his name. Timmy had just brought me
this bird dog I wanted to try out. Beautiful dog. Name
is Willy.

We had a fair morning. Found two coveys. Willy did
beautiful. Lunchtime, I pulled the pickup under some
trees off the long dirt road between Farley and Hill
View. I like the stopping for lunch about as good as the
hunting, you want to know the truth. We had sardines
and beans and some cans of Red, White & Blue. I
bought some hot sauce for the sardines.

He starts in telling me about this uncle of his—traveled

around with fairs and all that, circuses and stuff. Might be coming to see him before too long. That's how we got into my endangered-species thing.

"You know," I said, "you can't hardly have a circus now with all these cruelty-to-animal people all over the place. You use a whip and a chair in that tiger's cage and you liable to get arrested."

"That's right," he says.

"If somebody tells me I can't feed my family because of a goddamned turtle . . ."

He forked a sardine, shook off the oil. Looked at me like what are you talking about?

"I'm talking a turtle," I said. "I got friends in Morehead City their family's going hungry because some goddamned *sea* turtle is a so-called endangered species. Their *live*lihood is endangered—my friends' I mean. That's what's endangered. You see what I mean?"

"Yeah." He spooned some beans. Didn't seem all that interested. This is serious business down on the coast.

"What I want to know," I said—I get pretty worked up about this stuff—"what I want to know is how the hell they going to *count* all them goddamned sea turtles. Huh? I mean there's a lot of ocean out there. And what you see is only the top. Know what I mean? What you see is only the top. And let's say just for argument, let's say they all *do* die. So what? There's plenty of pictures of them. And films of them. Why should a man's livelihood be endangered because a damn *sea turtle's* endangered. That looks like to me it's putting the horse before the cart. Huh? We're talking a human being and his family's *live*lihood. I mean this man, this friend of mine, had his job before any of them big-ass sea turtles ever got endangered. I mean first things first. Fair is fair. Really. And what we're talking about anyway is the whole *species* being endangered. Not just that one turtle. See what I mean?''

He said he did—seemed a little more interested. ''I mean I can see regulations, though,'' he said.

Notice I hadn't said anything about regulations.

''You got to have regulations,'' he says, ''but it does get ridiculous when you start messing with a man's livelihood. That means you're messing with his family. I mean he might have kids and all that.''

''That's right,'' I said. ''God expects you to take care of your own.'' I spooned some beans. ''If there is a God.'' My jaw was popping like it does sometimes. I got this bad jaw. It pops everytime I chew. Sometimes I notice, sometimes I don't. Out there in the woods it seemed loud for some reason.

I do believe there is a God, but in any case, I got it figured out, so I says, ''Let's say there *is* a God. Okay. Now. Look at Mother Nature. You got animals killing other animals all over the place. Huh? You got birds killing insects. Animals killing birds. Insects killing insects. Birds killing birds. Hell, insects killing animals. Now, all this is one of the laws of God, else it wouldn't be *happening* all over the place. So you have to think about this: does God expect man to be any different? Why, hell no. Of course not.''

I let that sink in. I could tell he was thinking. He was sucking down those sardines, too. He wouldn't use any hot sauce, though. I tried to get him to.

''Now, on the other hand,'' I said, ''let's say there

ain't no God. Okay? Okay?'' He nodded. ''Well, in that case it don't make no difference about nothing. You can kill whatever you want to. See? See, I've spent some time thinking about this.''

''I can tell.''

''Either way it works.''

''Yeah, I see what you mean.''

Some people you talk this stuff to and they look at you like you're crazy. I think Faison was with me.

I walked a few steps into the woods, unzipped my pants, took a leak, waving old Rangatang in circles. The stream breaks up into great big drops. I like to watch it do that. I tucked myself back in, zipped up. One thing I like about the woods—you can piss where you want to. That's what I like about my yard, too. In my family we got a tradition of pissing in the yard— just the men, though. At least, as far as I *know* just the men. Huh? It makes you appreciate your freedom.

Faison was looking down, scraping his paper plate, scraping up some paper.

''I tell you one thing,'' I said. I waited. He looked up. ''What I do—and this is the bottom line—what I do is I treat people the way I want to be treated. That's what I do, and what I can't for the life of me understand is why people don't treat me the same way. Can you answer me that one?''

''No, I can't,'' he said. ''I sure can't.'' He turned up his beer can.

''It's a political world,'' I said. ''That's what I say. It's a political world. And I think it's a shame. You take my brother. It's politics that's kept him from getting the kind of medical benefits from the U.S. government that he ought to be getting. I think it's a shame.''

"It *is* a shame," he says. He pulls out a fresh toothpick from somewhere, asks me if I was in 'Nam, too.

"Oh yeah," I said. "Did you know 'Nam spelled backwards is man?" I could tell he hadn't thought about it. "But I have to say," I said, "my brother had it rougher than I did. But I had it rough enough. It's hard to explain to somebody that won't in it."

"Yeah," he says, and then he says, "And dog spelled backwards is god. Did you ever think about that?" A word man here. Then he tells about his brother being a fighter pilot in the navy and a cousin being a fighter pilot and a cousin getting a leg shot off and all this stuff. His brother teaches out at Ballard—could have been flying with the airlines.

I could tell he wanted to get off the deep stuff onto family stuff. That was okay.

"My brother's seven years younger than me," he said. "I about had to raise him. But he's the one had all the breaks. He deserves some credit, though. He won a Silver Star in 'Nam. He was a actual hero. The real thing. He just got through buying him a old airplane." He went on about his brother. He didn't talk none about his boy. Timmy told me he had a boy that died. I figured I wouldn't pry.

"Let's go shoot some quail," I said. "Here, have a cold one." People will talk about their families till the cows come home.

"Yeah," he says. "Right-o. Let's go."

And here this idea struck me. I'd been trying to figure out how to get to Hickory to get some rattlers without driving all day. It's getting damn hard to ship them anymore. So I asked him, "Think maybe your brother would fly me down to Wilmington or Hickory to buy some rattlesnakes?"

He said he probably would.

I have to get them from both ends of the state, and I swear I hate the driving.

"Won't hurt to ask him," he said. Then he got back into the family stuff. Talked about his brother having everything handed to him, all the good breaks and all that. I think maybe it's been the opposite with me and Timmy. Timmy's the one had the bad breaks, but my life ain't been no roller coaster, I can tell you that.

All in all, we had a good hunt. Willy did great. Smart as a whip. Pretty as a picture. Retrieved. The whole nine yards. I couldn't believe it. We got six birds. I got four and Faison got two. The dog is a dandy.

On the way back, Faison says, "Turn in this next driveway. I'll show you something." So I do and we go up this long driveway to a old white farmhouse. Pretty place. There were some old tobacco barns and stuff, and he says this was where he grew up and that if his stepmother died before his daddy—they were both sick—he and his brother would get the whole place. I know something about what land's going for over there—it's within a couple of miles of TechComm—so I figure this Faison is a possible future millionaire. No small bacon. And he's the kind of guy I wouldn't mind being friends with. See, so if it all works out we might be doing some fishing and hunting in Australia or somewhere.

We're turning the truck around to leave and he says,

"Look-a yonder," and I'll be damned if this airplane ain't landing right behind the house.

It was his brother he'd been telling me about. We walk on out there and damn if this little blue-and-white airplane ain't a beauty. Built in 1946. He landed it right there in this field behind the house.

I forgot to ask him if he'd take me to get some snakes. That would be great if he would. Hickory and Wilmington. That's where my contacts are. I swear I hate the drive. It's lots shorter now that I-40 is open to Wilmington but it would still be nice if I didn't have to do it.

The brother had a goddamn hippy with him. Turned out to be his boy. Huh?

6

Faye

I WAS HAPPY THAT THE WEATHER WAS FINALLY GET-
ting warmer. The bare trees along I-85 from Charlotte
to Summerlin budded with that kind of faint green mist
that I love so much.

I met Tate at the 7-Eleven the way I always do—first
Friday afternoon of every month. He paid his and Faison's part of a month's salary for Gloria, food, diapers,
the night sitter, and other necessities. We exchanged a
few words. I bought a bottle of tomato juice as usual,
and Tate bought his Diet Sprite and pack of Nabs. The
meeting was brief, ritualistic, as if we were from different countries. I get tired of this, but I can't imagine
it will last much longer. One of them has to die soon.

And if I end up with the homeplace I'll have to come back here to settle things with those boys who will be unhappy and their aunts who will be unhappy. Their position, according to the Fullers, is that it shouldn't become Mother's because she never "worked" the land. All this regardless of the wishes of my stepfather, the owner. In other words, inheritance laws are invalid, somehow, even though my stepfather bought the land and now wants his wife to have it because of the unselfish care she gave him for nine or ten—eleven?—years. The sisters apparently believe that there is some kind of feudal right they have by virtue of prior occupancy and the amount of time they spent "working" the place. I fail to see it, and thank goodness the wisdom of the law does not recognize that line of reasoning.

Driving up the long driveway to the homeplace—after the 7-Eleven—I first saw the familiar green Ford truck, and then I saw, sitting on the front porch, Mrs. and Mr. Fuller, perennial visitors, bearing a vague resemblance to vultures.

I did not want to sit and talk to these people, these people who would visit Mercury if someone were sick there—they'd endure the heat for the sake of a visit— these salt-of-the-earth people Mother did used to like so much, while she still had her mind. These people who seem interested in Charlotte and the law in such a way that I know they disapprove, or at least can't understand that a *woman* could get a law degree, move away to Charlotte, and then *stay* there after her mama gets sick—and still not harbor a callous soul. And besides all that, be as old as I am without a *husband*.

Sometimes I fantasize about putting people like this on the stand and asking them questions—for days—until I find out exactly why, what line of reasoning they use, why they believe so strongly in one narrow, bent moral code for all peoples on earth. If you planted them among the Arabs, then within six weeks they'd be cutting off thieves' hands left and right. I know they would.

But also, I can't deny that there is a kind of comforting steadfastness about them.

As I started up the front porch steps, they were both ready, brimming. She was sitting, rocking energetically, smiling at me, and he was leaning forward, his elbows on his knees.

"Well hey, Faye," she said. "Miss Laura's looking a little better today. Didn't you think so, Harold?"

"Yeah," said Mr. Fuller. "She seemed to have a little more color today—or something. She shore ate the hell out of another box of candy." He leaned back comfortably. You'd think he lived there.

"Well, that's good," I said, "about the color anyway. But it's probably not a good idea to leave her with chocolate, unattended."

"I think you're right about that," said Mr. Fuller. "I tried to tell Wilma."

"No, you didn't," she said.

"Yes, I did."

"No, you didn't." She turned to me. "How long you going to be able to stay, Faye?"

"I'll be going back tomorrow afternoon. The usual."

"Which one you reckon is going to die first?" said Mr. Fuller, leaning forward again, looking at me.

I stood with one foot on the top step, one foot on the

porch. You might think Mr. Fuller's question was unusual. It wasn't.

"Harold," said Mrs. Fuller.

"I don't know, Mr. Fuller," I said. "I just don't know. I'd hate to have to guess."

"That Gloria is bound to be right expensive," said Mr. Fuller.

"Well, she is," I said. "But at least she's dependable. I'm glad Tate is willing to help out."

"Poor Faison ain't moved a house in I don't know how long," said Mrs. Fuller. "That I know of. I don't imagine he can help out at all."

"Well—"

"If you get this place, you planning to hold it or sell it?" Mr. Fuller asked me.

"Harold."

"I really haven't thought that far ahead," I said. "I've been so busy. But you know, as I understand it—and apparently you do, too—it does depend on who dies first, you know, who gets the land and all."

I moved toward the front door, hoping this conversation might die.

"I was just thinking you'd surely get it all if Mr. Glenn goes, *then* Miss Laura," said Harold. "But if your mama happens to die first, and I certainly hope she don't—well, I hope neither one of them dies first—but, you know what I mean. If your mama dies and then Mr. Glenn dies it'll get interesting because my understanding is that he ain't got no will, and that Miss Bette and Miss Ansie ain't going to give up a portion of it without a fight. And now that Tate's landing that airplane out there all the time, and planning to build a hangar, you know he ain't going to want to sell."

I had the screen door open.

He says, "You know Prince Thackery sold his farm for eighty thousand dollars a acre. I wish to hell I'd bought a few acres twenty or thirty years ago. Eighty thousand dollars a acre."

"That's a whole lot," I said. I didn't know what else to say. It's the kind of conversation I find myself in around here—feeling stranded, like you stop at an intersection and find the intersection flooded. The car knocks off, you get out, and there you stand. Nowhere to go.

"I think I'll go on in and see how they're doing," I said. "It's good to see y'all again."

"Somebody ought to do something with that bird in there, Faye," said Mrs. Fuller. "The poor thing is going to freeze to death. I'd do something, but I don't want to, you know, intrude. Used to be it was just a few feathers gone from his neck. Now he's half-naked."

Inside Mother's room, I saw that it was true. Tiny, white-tipped pimples stood on Florida's yellow skin, a feather here and there, some fuzz, but the bird was mostly bare around the shoulders. He was getting worse. Most of his upper half was without feathers. His neck was as thin as a pencil. Blood had hardened under one wing where the skin was torn.

"Good gracious, Mama," I said. "Florida is not getting any better. He's getting worse, in fact."

Mother looked at the bird, held out her hand for me.

"He doesn't look well at all, Mama," I said. "And his toenails need cutting."

Mother spoke haltingly, quietly: "Wilma cut my toe-nails the other day." I have to admit that Mrs. Fuller is really good about that kind of thing.

"No, the *bird's*," I said.

"He don't . . ."

"What?"

"He don't talk no more," she whispered.

"Well, I don't guess he does talk anymore. I'm going to take him to the vet. I wish those boys would do something around here. I swear. It's their daddy's bird, too."

Gloria was getting ready to leave and I didn't see why she couldn't take Florida to the vet. I placed an old black skirt from Mother's closet—a closet still full of shoes and dresses from the last forty years or so—around the bird cage, put it on the front porch, and asked Gloria to take him in. She's good about things like that.

Gloria

You'd think that new Ballard College vet school that they made such a fuss over would work on birds, but they don't. There ain't but one vet in a hundred miles works on birds around here—Faye called all over the place—and his office was closed cause they was redoing it on the inside. So they had the whole thing set up in a house trailer in a field out beside their building.

So I walk up this little wheelchair ramp with this bird, thinking to myself the whole time, This here is how my life ending up. These here are my duties: taking Miss Laura Bales' sick bird to the bird doctor. It got me to feeling a little low.

My calling was to take care of peoples, not birds.

And if Miss Laura die while I'm up here, Faye will be there to get the credit of seeing her through, after all I done these last years, and I'll be in this here trailer with this bird.

About time I turn the doorknob to go in I want you to know that bird says, "What are you *doing*?"

I tell him, I say, "Taking you to the bird doctor, you crazy thing."

Inside this trailer was a *mess*. Cardboard boxes all over the floor. A great big bird cage at the end of the trailer had this big old parrot and he screeched out, scared me to death. Florida went to fluttering around under Miss Laura's black skirt—what fluttering he could. I should say bumping, naked as he is.

I sat in the one empty chair. This man sitting beside me with this cage holding a hungry-looking cat says, "You realize a parrot like at costs upards of two thousand dollars?"

"No, I didn't," I said. Why would I know that?

"I wouldn't have one if you *give* it to me," he says. He goes on about them killing his ears. "I wouldn't have one of them things if you *give* it to me," he keeps saying, just talking away like he was on drugs.

This woman in a white doctor coat come in from the back. She look just like a parrot in the face.

And right then I thought again, This here is how I'm ending up my life, living with the birds. Going down the home stretch taking care of Miss Laura's bird. It made me feel right heavy.

The parrot-woman say to me, "Yes?"

"I'm bringing this bird in," I say, "for Mrs. Laura Bales."

"Yes. Let's see." She had a big ledger book on the table. "Florida? We haven't seen Florida in three years. Good gracious." She walked over and pulled up the black skirt on the cage. "My lord," she said. She talk some baby talk and then say, "He could freeze."

"I suppose he could," I said. "But where he stay it's usually plenty hot."

She took him on back in the back somewhere, and pretty soon she come back and say what Faye expected, that they going to have to keep him a couple of days and try to get his strength up. She say that he were a very sick bird, that if they tried to cut his toenails he liable to die.

Glenn

Gloria carried off the bird. I don't know why Laura ever wanted that bird. Mama and Papa never allowed any animals in the house.

I see my sisters, dressed in white, setting the basket with baby Tate in it at the end of a corn row. I'm just home from Wadesboro. It's a Friday afternoon. Faison is standing there, dressed in white. They're all dressed in white. Spring planting. Mama is back at the house and Papa is in another field somewhere, and we're all of us together making a living with no outside help from anywhere in the world. Dressed in white. And there's no choice in the world in the years to come when I get home on weekends—from Wadesboro or Salisbury—but to, of course, whip Faison for all he's done wrong, and to whip Tate for all he's done wrong. Spare the rod and spoil the child. When I get out of the car, after driving up the long driveway, and step inside the front room, I'm torn between the already-in-my-nostrils smell of food cooking in the kitchen—cabbage, corn bread, fried fatback—and the dark dread of my duty to the boys, to Faison and Tate. And to Papa.

"Well," Ansie would say, "they got in the pond yesterday. Both of them. And Faison got in the pantry before prayer meeting Wednesday night and turned on the molasses faucet and let it all run out in the floor. We got up what we could but it was one big mess."

And then it would be a matter of catching them so I could whip them. If I didn't whip the boys for doing wrong then there would be a great worry around in the air, a great uncertainty. If I didn't whip them, *I* might be whipped, still, by Papa, who was as serious and stern as God Himself. Papa feeling like whipping me would be as bad as him actually doing it because Papa's bad feeling would bring me to shame at what I would be doing to him, hurting him, shaming him, putting him in such a fix that he might crumble apart, fly apart, in front of my eyes.

You know, about Papa. He could always stand hard field work. He was a real man. He could bring his raging up to the surface, but it seems to me now when I think on it that he couldn't somehow stand any other feelings rising up to the surface. That's the way he had to be. All that other was never there because it would have made him weak somehow, you see. It would have. He was steady, a rock. That way he could keep his bearing. We all needed him to keep his bearing, his power. Even now we all need that. Even now that he's dead.

I think I kind of worship—or something—them all, standing there, all dressed in white, working in the fields, tending crops, plowing, cutting wood and bringing it in, walking down to the spring and bringing back cool butter and milk. And this must have been the same with Mama and Papa. They must have remembered the ones before them that way. What would that boy of Tate's—I can't remember his name—what would that boy remember? And didn't Faison have one? What would he remember?

"Gloria, Gloria . . . Gloria, look at those little rivers up there in the ceiling, running side by side, straight.

Don't tell nobody this. Those boys were awful to me. And don't tell nobody, but I think about Evelyn more than I do Laura. I have to. I still burn with hate. It looks like after all these years some of it might go away and I know it's wrong to hate—almost fifty years, almost half a whole century of it—but I hate her just the same, and I realize that the hate is piled up on the love, and the love can't get out, can't get no air. I did love her before I hated her. I don't know where she went when she left, what she did, who she lived with, how she died—if she has died. Bette said one time what she had heard. But what Bette heard was not right. It couldn't be. Back then I had never heard a word, seen a word or picture that could in any way account for that kind of love between any two women in the world. And I know Evelyn hadn't. There hadn't been any rumors of that kind of love that I ever knew about, no jokes about it, no inkling that a world created by God would tolerate such an evil and squalid abhorrence. It couldn't be called love.''

Tate

I looked from the front porch at the homeplace across the yard at the jonquils, buttercups, patches of new green grass. It was nice—had my feet propped up on the railing. The sun's rays slanted across the yard, through the trees, burning a kind of gold on the tree bark. In the edge of the woods was a dogwood tree with white petals. The air was fresh. It was all very nice.

"Right pretty, ain't it," I said to Faison. He sat on the steps. We were holding down the fort while Gloria went to get Florida from the vet.

"You know what you ought to do?" he said, oblivious. He doesn't get into scenery. "You ought to take some time off sometimes. Go fishing and stuff. When Uncle Grove comes, we at least ought to take him fishing. Me and Jimmy are supposed to go fishing, anyway."

"He's going to want to see his gravesite—with the footstone," I said. "Why don't we go ahead and get a blank footstone put out there for you or me—in our section. One of us will need it first. We just split the cost and the first one dies gets it. We just don't write anything on it now—just put it there in the Bales section. Low-key, don't say anything. And then when Uncle Grove comes and wants to see his spot we just lay that brass plate on it and he'll think it's his. Then if he dies we can worry about that then."

"I got a better idea," said Faison. "I already figured it out. When they call and say they're dropping him off, I'll take the brass plate out there and lay it down on top of Ma Laura's and Daddy's footstone since there ain't no grave there yet, and then when we take him out there he'll think that's his. My way is simpler."

"How do you know that brass plate will fit?"

"I can tell by looking at it."

"What if somebody dies—Daddy or Ma Laura?" I said. "A lot could happen in the next three weeks."

"Then we'll do your plan. But, hell, we could put that brass plate anywhere. And then as soon as he's seen it, we'll take it up. Simple. It'll be down just one day and nobody will ever know but him and us. And you know good as I do that Bobbie and Four-Eyes are gone have him cremated in Arkansas. They're Episcopalians."

"I don't know about that. I told her I'd come get his body. It wouldn't cost her anything."

"What would you do, ride him up front with you?"

"I don't know," I said. "I'd rent a U-Haul."

"Shit, Tate. Anyway, worse comes to worse he could be buried in one of those plots over there beside Junior."

Gloria drove up and got out with Florida in his cage under some kind of black cloth. "He's already talking some," she said, carrying him on in. "He got him a new lease on life."

"Somebody should have fed him to the cat," said Faison. Then he started in again about a fishing trip. The thing about Faison is, he'll get all up for doing something like that and then it'll just drop.

"It's going to be probably sometime in the middle of the summer before I finish this project I'm working on," I said. "This is overlapping with some other things I got going. Maybe we can go fishing in the fall."

"Seems like they all overlap," he said. "I never knowed one of your projects to finish."

"Yeah, they kind of do overlap, usually. One thing leads to another. You got to hook it up to something—

a grant or something—if you want to get any money out of it.''

"We get this place," he said, "you won't have to worry about money no more. We sell this place and you can *buy* a airport. This ain't no good for a landing strip.''

"It's a perfect place for a landing strip. And this land has been in the family," I said.

"You're crazy, Tate."

"Listen," I said. "Faye has got as much chance of getting this place as we do."

He started in on how much Faye and Marilyn are alike, and wanted to know what kind of problems I was having with Marilyn now.

I told him none, that Morgan was the problem now.

"You never whipped his ass enough," he says. Faison says that about once a month.

"Maybe so."

"He ain't too old yet."

"I wish I could get him some summer work."

"That's what you needed. Work. Work, work, work. You got babied."

"I worked on the farm. Get off it."

"What'd you do? Tie tobacco a few times? Pick a few ears of corn?"

"I hear you, Faison." There is stuff Faison will never turn loose.

"No problem," he says. "There's a baby in every family. It ain't your fault."

He loves running this stuff in the ground.

Gloria came to the porch door. "Y'all's daddy wants to see you," she said.

Inside we stood on opposite sides of Daddy's bed. The railings were up. The room smelled bad. I pulled back the sheet and looked. There was a new smell, a smell like sour urine and something else, sharp, rancid, vinegary. He was so damn helpless.

"I just changed him," said Gloria, standing in the doorway. "When I get that garbage bag out, it'll smell better in here. You know?"

"Open that window," I told Faison. Then to Gloria, "Think maybe you could get it out now?"

Daddy's lips quivered. He started crying. He brought his hand to his head. The gown dropped from his arm. His elbow looked like a gray, unlit light bulb and his arm was thin. He held his hand just above his eyes. His fingers shook. "I didn't want it to . . . I didn't want it to be like this." He looked from Faison to me, locked his eyes on me. "I wish you-all would just go in there and talk to her a minute or two, Son . . . and see how she's doing." He glared at me—a kind of hard glare, panicked. "She's always been so good to me. I was lucky to find somebody like her. God has been good to me. You boys just never . . ."

Faison dropped his hands from the bed railing, turned, walked back over to the open window. It was getting to him.

From down the hall came this voice: "Harold, you know it ain't so."

"Who was that?" said Daddy. "I didn't know nobody was here."

"The bird," I said. "Gloria took him in, got him drugged up or something."

108

"Tate, oh Tate," Daddy wailed. He dropped his hands to his sides. "I got bedsores, Son."

"I'm sorry, Daddy," I said. "I just . . ."

"She won't ever good to me," said Faison. "That's the problem. The fact is, she treated me like dirt."

"Oh, no, no," wails Daddy. "Evelyn's the one did that."

"No, she didn't," says Faison. "She didn't treat me like dirt."

"She *left* you. She deserted you, Faison. And she deserted Tate. And she deserted me."

"She never treated me like Ma Laura did," said Faison. "That's for sure."

"Laura has done everything she could for you, Son. You just wouldn't ever let yourself appreciate it." He started crying. His hands were over his face, his body shook in the bed. It tore at me.

"You couldn't pay me to go in there," said Faison.

"I guess she had her own problems, too," I said.

"Shit," Faison said to the grass outside the window. I could see that the grass was in the shade and the only sunlight was weak at the top of the trees. The sky was light green, and down across the field you could see the weak gray-yellow horizon. It was like we were at the end of something. Nothing was going to change. There was no way.

Then Daddy stopped crying, and he pulled his hands away from his face. "Don't you talk like that in here, Faison," he said. "And that's right. That's right. She had her own problems, too. Did you even hear what Tate just said?"

"I heard him. But I ain't going in there. She wouldn't

come in to see me if I was sick. She wouldn't come to see me if I was dead. And you know that as good as I do, and you know what else, Daddy? You took it. You *took* it. You took it all laying down.'' Faison turned from the window and started toward the bed. I was afraid he might grab Daddy. But he just yelled at him. ''You wouldn't a bit more stand up to her than nothing. You was afraid of her. Goddamn, that was it, and you know—''

''Stop it! Stop it!'' Daddy was yelling, even as weak as he was. ''Don't you curse me,'' he said. ''You never helped nothing work out, Faison. I couldn't help I had to work. You were mean to her. You left. You don't have a right to—''

''*Right?*'' Faison turned half away, then back. ''After working my ass off on this place until I was sixteen years old? And then I catch it because I don't go to *college*. Come off it. Don't talk to me about what I don't have a *right* to. I worked my *ass* off on this place.''

Daddy held up his hand, looked at me, kept talking to Faison. ''You can't even hold a job. Just be quiet.'' Then he said to me, ''Would you go in there and see her, Son?'' He turned on that hard glare—part command, part plea.

I looked at Faison. ''No, I don't think so, Daddy.''

Faison walked out, slammed the door behind him.

Daddy's hands were at his face again. He was crying.

''I got to be getting on, Daddy,'' I said. ''I'm sorry about all this. Try not to think about all that stuff. It's a pretty day outside. Spring is coming.''

Evelyn

And then I met Honour Walters. It was like this. She had come from New York for a wedding. She was originally from England. It was a fancy wedding and she had been sitting behind a table licking icing from her fingertips when I saw her, saw the shape of her face, Mary Magdalene, a soft Spanish look with a soft Spanish nose with a very slight little bump on its bridge, black eyes, and black, long, shiny hair, a dimple in her chin, and her soft white shoulders against the black, black hair, and I felt no choice in this wide world but to leave Glenn's side and walk around that table and—short of breath from the excitement—kid this woman, make a joke about her licking her fingers: "Don't you know this is a high-class wedding?" I asked. I felt the go-ahead to look at her, all over her, wherever I might have the slightest inclination to look, and there were inclinations to say whatever I wanted to, whatever was ready to come out, inclinations to look at the soft skin that continued on down out of sight, the rounded mounds with the tiny down smooth against the skin, the soft breasts under white cotton. I didn't know if at that moment I could stand the way I was feeling. I knew something had collapsed inside me as soon as I saw those fingertips in her mouth, saw her face, and whatever it was that collapsed was about to re-form and bolt, had to.

Glenn is bound to have delivered the boys to his mama that morning we left. He wouldn't have done anything else and she was sure as the world sitting out on that front porch shelling peas when he drove up. I don't think he would walk across the field with them. Too much trouble. I imagine he put them in the car, drove them by the driveway, and then went on to Salisbury.

I was by that time riding along in Honour's car, already missing the smells, including that other smell, that sweet smell of a baby just out of a bath and dried off. All I knew was that I had felt the falling in my chest, the falling, falling, falling to perhaps my death, the last breath, and knowing that while I was falling, the edge of the cliff higher and higher above me, that I wouldn't wake up because I was already awake. Those boys were left there behind with those sisters of Glenn's, with Glenn's mother who never did *not* suggest what to feed them, how to feed them, what to dress them in, and how; left with the thicket—it seemed, though there were only two—of sisters, their hands all over the boys, mocking punishment, taking both boys out of my sight down behind the barn at the same time while I sat on the porch with his mother, forcing talk about who was, who wasn't at church that day, who did, who didn't speak ugly words, who did, who didn't drink a toddy now and then, who did, who didn't . . . you name it.

My mistake, one of them, had been to dream of moving to town. With Glenn. Any town. And I dreamed of washing his clothes and hanging them out and folding them and putting them away and cooking for him and setting food before him on the table of a little house in town, but while having the library and clubs nearby. I never guessed that I might drown in something besides water, drown dead in secret *love* with this woman Honour Walters who talked with the clean strong accent from England and who whispered when she talked to me about ME and who was crazy about me, who had fallen in love with me, ME, touched me, said my name over and over, and then kept touching me and touching me and touching me until I could not live another day without the touch, physical, and whatever all else there was. I had to decide to ride in that car, with her driving, straight away from my two sons and that life. Shame settled on me like soft black snow, but lifted and melted away when I looked at Honour. Honour was life away from the thicket. I knew that my own life had become mired in a rhythm, a system on that farm that was the dark side of the moon—mud and heavy curtains falling in front of my face every day, unannounced. Weights hung from my arms. I'd begun to see that life in town would never happen. Glenn was bound to the farm, to his mother and father, brothers and sisters. Bound in a way he was never bound to me, bound with thick cords, while his binding to me was with tiny, weak strings. I could leave with Honour Walters, warding off the shame. Or I could stay, not leave with Honour Walters, and drown dead perhaps, and still lose the boys to those people anyway.

If I took the boys, I'd be chased down. If I didn't, they'd let me go.

Honour told me over and over that I shouldn't do it, leave my family, that she Honour couldn't promise me anything but travel and no connections to anything but to her, that she was afraid I would somehow tire of her. I said I had no choice, that there was no choice to be made, that it was not a choice between taking one path or the other—Honour on the one hand, or Glenn and the kids on the other—that in fact there was no choice about my leaving. About choosing Honour. It was like . . . rain. It had come and you couldn't do anything about it. I know you can't believe that. But it's true. Believe me, it's true.

Honour had come to the wedding of her college roommate who was marrying a furniture man from North Carolina. She drove all the way down from New York where she was working. And there while she was waiting for the reception to be over, eating cake, I walked up to her. She had in the past—she told me later—been able to love all human bodies, all forms, all legs, torsos, arms, hands, feet, and many dispositions. I had, too, and I had fought it down with a vengeance—successfully, not understanding it was anything but evil—all my life. I'd fought it down with religion, then psychology, then shame, then logic, and I was holding it down with a sheer force of will when Honour came along and that heavy banner, laid down over my potential love and yearning, was lifted into the wind and blown away. I tried to hold on to it in the wind, but it was torn from my hands, and I was left naked, and hungry for her.

She was hit between the eyes, too, she said, knocked down to her knees. She told me that she could not walk away and not love me, there in the clean little community way down there in North Carolina, away from the commerce, chaffing, haggling, swapping, bartering of New York. But she couldn't ask me to go with her.

And she couldn't ask me not to go with her.

That day at the wedding, she had walked out into the front yard where others were gathered. I had followed.

"This is hot weather," she said.

"It is, isn't it."

"Did you grow up around here?" she asked.

"Down the road a ways. It gets bad in the summertime, especially July and August."

"I think I rather like it in a way," she said. "It's very human somehow. No, that's not the word. It's very . . . something."

"It's pleasant in the mornings, after a night rain."

"Do you have a family?" she asked me.

"I've got two boys and a hundred in-laws."

"Do you ever get away?"

"No."

"Do you ever want to?"

"Yes."

We stopped along the road and had some sandwiches made and put them in a white paper bag—Honour kept white paper bags—and then we drove until we found a dirt road and then a field with a cart path. We took a blanket out and sat under a tree, eating sandwiches and drinking cold orange juice, fresh squeezed and smelling good, and the june bugs were popping in the field and the boys weren't hanging all over me—for the first time, it seemed, in my life. The boys weren't in my face, between my legs, at my elbow, and the pull deep inside me—for my children—was relieved by the popping of the june bugs, the sight of Honour sitting there on the blanket, already unbuttoned some. I forced everything that was wailing and rearing up to a place behind me. I forced it all down, though it did, at times, rise up and overcome me. Honour was always there to help me regain myself.

You see, don't you, that my husband Glenn had never, ever told me that he *loved* me. Do you see what I was up against, what I was in? But Honour could talk about love. She could flat talk about love. She quoted Shakespeare, Song of Solomon, and others.

And I knew that if Honour disappeared, even for a minute, I would be draped, suffocated in a black guilt. And I knew that as long as she was there, I would have a happiness that rode herd on all that back there behind me where those two boys would get more attention— surely they would—than they could handle. And surely they'd have a chance to live on that farm. Even though they were my blood, they were their blood, too, and somehow all of it back there hadn't quite took. I hadn't took to it. I'd been repelled by it, and I never knew that until Honour came.

I decided that the boys would take, in time, to all those aunts and uncles and their grandma and grandpa. They had already took. They wouldn't miss me so much. I remembered, and have remembered over and over again, the Mama-Papa-Glenn-Bette-Ansie-aunts-uncles-cousins glob of mudclayglue. In the glob are the two small diamonds that are my boys. But I keep them covered. If they are about to shine through I run my fingers over the mudball, shaping it so the diamonds are covered again and again.

And Glenn was such a baby. Such a baby.

Part Three

You're History
Longer Than
You're Fact

7

Gloria

SUNDAY MORNINGS I DON'T COME IN UNTIL TEN. RE-
lieve the teenager. Last Sunday morning, Mrs. Fuller
drove up same time I did. She was on the way to church,
stopping by to check on Miss Laura. Time we got in
the door, we could hear Florida saying "Nut 'N Honey"
over and over. I liked him better with his mouth shet.
The teenager was out the door like a cat. She always
that way.

While I put up my things, Mrs. Fuller, with her handful of Kleenex, kind of dawdled into Miss Laura's room,
where she stay about fifteen seconds, then she come
shuffling out like a trotting mule. *"Lord,"* she say.

119

"Lord almighty," she shout, *"she's dead, she's dead! Lord gosh almighty."*

It had happened. I stopped at the phone, picked up the receiver, and pushed 911. "We got a mergency," I said. "Somebody passed. Turner Road, first driveway on the right past the Antique Mart."

They want to know how long she been dead and who I was.

I said I didn't know, and that I was the practical nurse.

That teenager. Marsha What-ever. I knew it. She supposed to check in on both of them at bedtime, in the night, and next morning. I bet she ain't done none of that.

Well, finally. This look like it mean them boys was going to get the place, when all this time it been looking like it gone be just the opposite.

I was already checking the wall list for Faye's number.

"Miss Faye, it look like your mama have passed," I said.

She say, "What?"

"Passed away."

"Is this Gloria?"

"Yes'um."

"She's what, Gloria?"

"*Dead*. She just *died*."

"Oh no."

"Yes ma'am, a few minutes ago. That's what Mrs. Fuller say. I'm real sorry."

"Was Mrs. Fuller with her?"

"No ma'am. She was in there by herself. We called mergency and they're sending a amulance."

"Does Mr. Bales know yet?"

"No'um, we ain't tole him but I imagine he heard the racket."

Then I called Faison and Tate but neither one of them home. I was stalling, hoping Miss Wilma had gone in to tell Mr. Glenn. Lord have mercy, I hated to do that.

When I hung up, I looked toward Mr. Glenn's room. Mrs. Fuller stood there in the door with her back brace up against the doorjamb. She start sliding down to the floor, real slow. A tissue drop from her hand, then another one. Time I got to her she was sitting on the floor, with her head tilted back. She was fully fainted, passed out. Gone.

Mr. Glenn, see, he was dead, too.

Faye

As soon as I got off the phone with Gloria, I drove to Summerlin. I realized as I drove that I was less prepared, emotionally, than I thought I was. The farm would, of course, go to Faison and Tate. Well . . . I could turn that loose. But Mother deserved something other than her meager final rewards. She took care of Glenn so long.

I walked into a houseful of visitors—all just out from church, I'm sure. As soon as I got into the hallway I stopped, brought my hands to my face. A dark lead blanket had dropped over me.

Mrs. Fuller walked up and put her hand on my shoulder, then hugged me. I hugged back. I almost loved her for a minute.

Then I stood there thinking, Why can't I just get in and get out? Why can't I just get in and sign a paper and get it over with, have the funeral, get back to Charlotte, back to work, and remember what my mother and real father and life were all like when I was growing up. Why can't I just grieve alone, and not have to put up with those boys, those aunts, and all that. It was enough knowing that Tate and Faison would end up with the whole place.

"Oh, Faye," said Mrs. Fuller, "she was such a wonderful lady. We're all going to miss her. But I know none of us will miss her like you do." She tried to hand me one of those Kleenex tissues. I refused it.

"And we ain't got no way of knowing which one died first," she said.

"What? When?"

"First."

"First what? I didn't . . ."

"Died."

"Do you mean . . . Are you telling me that Mr. Bales died, too?"

"No. What I was telling you was we ain't got no way of knowing which one died first."

"Who?"

"Your mama or Mr. Bales."

"Mr. Bales died, *too*?"

"You didn't know that?"

"NO."

It was as if the room suddenly started spinning. Two deaths had occurred in the same night. My own dear mother and this man, her husband. Besides all the immediate, complex confusion was the fact that I was suddenly in the middle of some kind of inheritance nightmare with those Bales brothers.

I had to sit down and get my breath.

Wilma Fuller

They must have died at the same time. That teenager is no-count. Of course, both of them dying like that, something fishy could have been going on, but I ain't going to mention that unless somebody else does.

Faye was right distraught, of course.

It all took my breath. I fainted. But that ain't the first time. Someday I'm going to sit down and write down all the times I've fainted.

I just discovered them—one, then the other. I walked into Miss Laura's room and there she was sitting up, dozing, I thought, leaning a little to one side, you know, like she sometimes got when we was visiting. Me or Harold used to push her back up straight. She looked just exactly like she was asleep. Then I walked over there to the bed and said, "Miss Laura, Miss Laura, are you asleep?'' Well, of course she didn't answer. She had gone to her reward. And Florida saw it all, bless his heart. I moved him out in the hall so he wouldn't have to be in there with her.

Next, I made the announcement, see, to Gloria. About Miss Laura. Gloria got on the phone and I went in to tell Mr. Glenn, of course—I hated to—and Lord almighty, he was dead, too. I declare if I didn't think he was sleeping hisself, but I said to myself as I walked over to the bed that for sure . . . I said Lord have mercy this could not happen twicet in the same day, lightning striking twicet. But, bless his heart, he was stone dead. And before I knew what was going on, Gloria was fanning me on the floor and Lord the rescue squad had to split up and work on both of them at the same time I reckon—I couldn't look . . . What do you reckon they do when somebody is already dead? I guess they relax. Slow down a little.

I sat on the porch while they was in there, and then that Murphy fellow, Percy Murphy's boy, youngest, called the funeral home—the boy that got his foot cut real bad in the county lawnmower that time at the schoolhouse—told them to bring two cars, that lightning had struck twicet.

Poor Faye. She was in such a tizzy. I have never really deep down liked her all that much, but those kinds of feelings just can't count when somebody loses their mama. I don't care if they're in prison, even. There's something about losing your mama that makes the kind of person you are not count at all.

I told Faye not to worry at all about food. I'd made

a few phone calls and the chicken and cakes and pies were already rolling in.

I asked Faye what she thought we should do with Florida. Maybe give him to Gloria? But she couldn't think about Florida right then, she said, and of course she was right. And right then Florida whistled and then said, "Harold, that's not so."

He says some of the funniest things. Harold says he sounds just like me. I say he don't. He says he does. Once that bird got well he started talking up a storm. Says anything he hears on TV—or anywhere else—that he decides he wants to say. I heard him say "Toyota" one time. They got more commercials than McDonald's.

Course the big question everybody is going to be asking I suppose, once all the grief dies down, is *who died first*?

I knew all about the funeral arrangements so I explained to Faye as carefully and gently as I could. The arrangements were for Mr. Glenn to be viewed there at the homeplace, and Miss Laura up at the funeral home. Then I wondered while I was talking if I had it backwards. But I told her, and I'm sure she knew this, that it *was* Claremont. And they are the best. Mr. Simmons had said for Faye to give him a call. He'll tell her who's going to be where.

Anyway, after the embalming, they were to deliver one back to the homeplace and leave the othern up there. With the circumstances like they are with the boys and all, I think where who wanted to be viewed had been planned out that way some time before. But with lightning striking twicet there would be, you know, hundreds of visitors. At least they were both in on the prearrangement plan, thank goodness.

We had Mr. Glenn's room for sitting since it was closest to the door. We aired it out—moved his bed out on the back porch. I bought a can of Pine Fresh. I told Faye that after all was said and done, her mama's room did smell better than Mr. Glenn's. I think she needed to know that. She said she appreciated it. I said I'd do it for anybody.

Me and Harold thought a lot of Miss Laura.

Nobody could get in touch with the boys, we thought, but then we figured out they had been notified, because Bert Talmadge said he'd seen them out at the graveyard with somebody—some old man, he said—checking out the burial plots. Mr. and Mrs. Bales have had a footstone already out there for a long time, so that won't be no problem. It pays to think ahead. I was glad the boys were taking care of that.

Faye got her a room at the Holiday Inn. Of course she couldn't stay in the homeplace under the conditions. One of the most embarrassing things I have ever encountered was right before she left. I have never. It would have been okay if it had happened after she left, but no, it had to happen right before she left, while she was standing there. That bird. He whistled, then this is what he said. He said, "Git yo ass on the pot, Miss Laura."

Grove

This was the place. Yes. I looked at my gravesite. It looked nice. There was green grass. The footstone. The big brass plate. "It meets my approval," I said.

I took a deep breath, relaxed. The boys were quiet. I looked around, over at the church. I remembered Anna's eyes when she stood beside that wood post that was in the cabin that was . . . "Where did that cabin used to be? The church cabin. Wadn't it right there under them trees?"

"I don't know," said Tate. "It was torn down before I was born, I guess."

"You never saw the church cabin?" I asked him.

"I think I remember it," said Faison. "It was right there."

Tate's boy was with us. Morgan.

Bobbie, Four-Eyes, and Tina were on the road to Washington, D.C., for a week. Good riddance. Now I could settle everything here.

I remembered the way Anna looked up at me—a kindness there in her eyes. Something I don't remember seeing since then in anybody's eyes, much less Tina's, who's been telling me for over a year now that I've lost my senses. I ain't lost nothing, unless it's my curveball.

"It's got kind of a view across that way," said Tate.

These boys have been good to me.

"It looks like Don's grave," I said. "The grass around here. The way the grass is. Don Wheeler. Had the little dog I despised." Good time for that story.

"We were riding along in his station wagon with all his kids one time, mess of kids, and that little dog, a poodle, with some kind of bow around its neck, was in the back with the kids. Right after station wagons come out. Had the wooden sides. Real wood. Stuff would get eat out by termites, you know. Little son-of-a-bitch dog would always snap at me is why I didn't like him. So I'm sitting up front with Don in the station wagon with all them noisy kids and so forth and so on and that dog in the back, and I want you to know that dog gets his collar hung over the back window handle, you know, to roll the window up and down with, and one of the kids screams, so I turn around and see what's happening and try to get him unhooked and the little son of a bitch snaps at me. Bares his teeth and snaps at me, like a little ole rat. Well, I say, 'Don, we'd better stop and get this dog off this handle back there,' and he says, 'What?' Kids are so loud."

I needed to set down, so I did—on a little stone wall close by. Faison and Tate set with me. The boy set on the ground. Hippy-looking. "Why don't you get your hair cut?" I asked him.

He shrugs. "I don't know."

"Well, one of them kids reaches over and grabs the dog, see, and can't get him loose, and when the kid drops him back, when he drops him back he flips him over, somehow, so that the collar tightens a loop, and the dog's eyes is popping out but he ain't making no noise. So he gives a little jerk and goes limp and the kids start screaming, and I'm looking at all this see, so I say, 'Don, I think you better pull over, your dog might be dead.' I was hoping the dog *was* dead. So Don pulls

128

over to the side of the road. And it's raining, see. I manage to get the dog off the handle—it's pretty easy now—and out the car and hand him to Don. The kids are all pressed up to the windows, and the rain is sprinkling down right steady, and Don is baldheaded, combs his hair up over the bald top, and all that hair is washed down over his ear, and his glasses are steamed up, and he's standing there in the rain holding this dead dog. And he goes to hand me the dog and says—and here you got to know I once brought a bird dog back to life with mouth-to-mouth, actually it's mouth-to-nose in the case of a dog . . . you know, whatever they call it. I had this reputation. So Don tries to hand me the dog and says, 'Bring him back to life, Grove. You know how to do it.' I don't take the dog. The rain starts picking up. The dog is good and dead and wet by now and looks like a long limp skinny hot dog. I said, 'You can do it as easy as I can.' The kids are pressed up against the window and screaming and crying, their noses all mashed in against the glass. Don sees I ain't gone do it. See, I'm *glad* the dog is dead.

"So he gets the dog up in his arms and cradles him like a baby, you know, and tries to figure out how to do it. I said, 'Just hold his mouth closed and puff through that little wet nose, then back off. Puff. Back off.'

"And he did. Dog would puff all up, then go down. Puff all up, then go down. Right off, in oh, eight to ten seconds, the damn dog kicks, jerks, and there he is: good as ever, squirming around trying to get down. Worrisome little rascal. Don was right proud of hisself. Don's funeral was the last I went to. So I'm saying this looks like Don Wheeler's gravesite. Y'all ready to go? I appreciate you taking care of this. I couldn't have done a better job myself. It's just where I want to be."

We started back toward the car. Passed right by that Valentine tombstone. I looked at it for a minute—the one me and Anna used to sit up against. Then we started walking again.

"Uncle Grove," said Tate, "I've got something I want you to see."

"What's that?" I said.

"It's a secret for now. It's about thirty minutes outside town."

Faison spills the beans, says it's a airplane. Tate gets mad at him.

"Do what?" I said. You have to keep saying that so they think you can't hear. Then when you don't want to listen you can just sit.

They fussed a little more. Turns out Tate's got a Super Cruiser. That's what I had. Nice little airplane. Got in my blood.

I flew mine off a pole. That's a long story. But a good one.

We got in the car. The young one looked like he might be just right to help me out. Hell, he was probably used to hiding stuff from everybody. Smoking cigarettes. Hiding magazines. He'd be just right. Helping old Grove pull one over on them. I had to have some help from somewhere.

When we got back to Tate's apartment—I was going to stay with him the first night anyway—we hadn't been there more than five minutes when the boys got the call that their daddy had finally died. And their stepmama. Poor old Glenn had been sick ten, twelve years.

Faison

This was unreal. Unreal. No way to have any idea who died first, as it was. I knew I had to act and act fast. Tate would sit on his ass. Faye would get to work with her fancy lawyer friends.

The thing that had to be found out was who died first. The land was joint ownership so that whoever died first meant the other one got it. So I knew we had to find out who died first.

You watch television, you know the way to find out when somebody died is with a autopsy.

Of course the trick is—here's the trick: I want to know who died first only if Ma Laura died first. See? Do you follow me? And if Daddy died first, I don't want to know. You get my drift?

The autopsies had to be done right away. I mean I can be sad later. I mean I am sad now, but I can be sad later, too. But you can't figure out who died first in a week or two. They need to be more or less still warm, I think, and if I don't find out right away, I'm thinking, then Miss Lawyer from Charlotte will be one up on me. She'll figure out some way to "finalize" something. Have you ever listened to the way they talk? Lawyers?

So I call Drew at the rescue squad. He more or less lives over there.

"Drew, what do you have to do to get a autopsy done?"

He tells me he's sorry about everything, and that I can get one done on Daddy because I'm next of kin, but not on Ma Laura.

Trouble. Right there.

"Look, Drew, I don't want Miss Laura's daughter, my stepsister, to know about the autopsies—I mean I need both of them done to find out who died first."

"I don't think you need a autopsy to find out when they died. You just examine the blood and then check out their core temperature. Something like that. But you'd need the daughter's approval for Mrs. Bales. Next of kin and all."

"Is there any way I could get around the daughter? It's real important, Drew."

"Well, yeah. Foul play. I mean foul play in their deaths. In that case the coroner would *order* autopsies and the medical examiner would do them, or have them done. Look, if you say I told you about all this, I'm denying it, okay? You need to understand that."

The plan bloomed beautiful in my head. I know the D.A., Gerald Smith. All I have to do is call him up and tell him I think the night sitter, one of the Blaine girls, murdered Daddy and Ma Laura in the night, but that she might not have, and I don't want to embarrass anybody, so could he keep the investigation secret. That way they'll have to do autopsies. But nobody would know. Then I can get Drew to find out which one of them died first. And with a little bit of luck, I'll be the only one outside the police who ever finds out, because hell, that night sitter didn't murder anybody, and then I can decide exactly how to release the information. It's a beautiful plan, all aboveboard, I mean, legitimate. Hell, she *could* have murdered them. It's possible. Anything's possible.

See, there was nothing to do but fight tooth and nail to hold on to the farm. It had all been screwed up since Mama left. If it wadn't for that, then things would have happened orderly—me and Tate would have got the farm, sold it, and I'd be a millionaire.

It sure as hell was *not* a good time for Uncle Grove to be around. I mean I was glad to see him, but he's always had a way of getting in the middle of things.

Grove

They had to go tend to funeral arrangements and all that and that left just me and the boy in the apartment.

Faison's boy's the one got killed in a car wreck. Tate's boy was the one with me and he wanted to know if I was in the war. Said his school class was doing a project.

I told him I missed out on all the military service,

but I wore a uniform for a while. World War I. Kept me out of some trouble. That's when I got started in the concession business—with fairs and the carnivals. I was in *those* wars. I had to shoot a fellow who was ripping up my tent with a knife one time. I told the boy about it. I yelled at this guy and he come at me and I shot him low, in the leg. Cost me sixteen dollars, doctor bill. Ah, boy.

Moon was behind the clouds that night, then out, then behind the clouds, then out. I ran you know, and got rid of the gun under a little wood walkway. Then snuck back around to where the crowd was gathered— I have always said you hide *in* the action—and they got the guy up off the ground and the moon all of a sudden came out from behind a cloud and he says, "There he is. There's the son of a bitch that shot me." So they put me in the can, and next morning the man I shot told the sheriff to make me pay the hospital bill and let me go. Why, today I'd been sued for everything I own.

"Yeah, and that's where I met up with my sister— your grandmama," I told him. "Up in them Kentucky mountains. It was about ten years after she left here. She'd seen my name in the newspaper—that I was in jail. She brought me some turnip greens, corn bread, country ham and biscuits, and preserves, and some cold buttermilk. She knew what I liked."

"My grandmother?" he says.

"That's right, your grandmother."

"Do you know where she is now?"

"Don't have no idea."

This boy was wearing a damn earring. There's no end to what they do nowadays. I told him a little bit about taking care of all that business about all that mess of his grandma's. Then I told him it was all off the record, so to speak. To forget I'd said it. I ain't ever been sure what all them boys know, what they don't know about their mama.

He wanted to know more, but I wouldn't let on. I told him some about the rough country up in and around them Kentucky coal mines. And I told him all about my game wheel.

I had fifteen, sixteen guys working for me, see. Some gambling stuff. I used to have a wheel with the pointer made like a snake, split in the very nose of it, with a little setscrew. And you take a piece of cigarette paper, newspaper, anything, put in there for the snake's tongue, and make a little pointer-arrow, you know. And you spin it, run it round and round this way. Like spinning the hand on a clock except it was all of one piece with the tail and head on either side of center. There was thirty-six nails in this one, in a circle around the outside, where the numbers on a clock would be. We had thirty-six spaces. And there were twenty-four open and twelve starred, to win on—so you had two-to-one odds.

And we're in a town up there on Snake River. Coal mine in there. And I told the boy exactly what happened.

"There was this guy up there had shot some guy a long time back in there on a carnival. And he walked up and wanted to know how the wheel worked. You pay a dime, turn it, and if it hits you win, so and so, and if it don't hit you lose. The whole setup had three legs to it."

I spread out three fingers like a tripod to try to explain it. It ain't easy to explain. I was trying to distract the boy a little from his granddaddy's dying but it didn't seem like he especially needed it. He was glued to the story.

I explained the mechanics of the wheel—how I could lean against this hollow two-by-four with a rod up the middle and control that pointer. It was actually a thing of beauty. I told him I could stop that pointer on a gnat's ass. I could, too.

"But I tell you what I did," I said. "I fired more than one guy for cheating old people. That's one thing I did not allow. You could not work for me and cheat old people—or women with children, that sort of thing, you know. I fired more than one.

"Anyway, this here fellow that come up, he got all stiff, and all blah, blah, blah, this, that, and the other, and I said, 'Well I just explained the game to you. And if you like it, play it, and if you don't,' I said, 'don't give me no argument.' I said, 'I don't care whether you play it or not.'

"Well he played for five, ten minutes, turning it as hard as he could every time, taking up a lot of time for just a little money, so I said, 'Listen, if you want to play some more it's going to cost you twenty cents and if you win you win double. And so he pulled out twenty cents. And a pistol. Cussing. He said it better win, so and so. Course when he did that I just reached under the counter and pulled out that big old forty-five I had back then and I said, 'I hope it does.' I said, 'If it *does*.' What I said—*he* said, 'It *better* win, or else'—I said, 'If it *does* I'm going to shoot you right between your eyes.' And he turned just as white as a sheet, Morgan, just as white as a sheet, stuck his gun in his pants, and walked off. Left his twenty cents right there on the counter."

The boy was, you know, taken with the story, I could tell. Probably a good boy, under all that hippy stuff.

He tried to tell me a little bit about computers. Then I just figured I might as well go ahead and tell him I needed some help on the little project I had to get done right away. He had his driver's license and I didn't figure those boys were going to want to help me, you know. Might be some resistance. So I told this one, Morgan, I'd pay him a hundred dollars to help me do something.

"Okay," he said.

"You don't want to know what it is first?" I asked him.

"Not especially. Either way."

"We might not be able to do it in one day. What it is, is this: I need to dig my grave and I need some help."

That backed him up a couple of steps.

"Look here," I said. Then I told him how I ain't gone get hooked up on no tubes and all that with them foreign juices flowing in my body from no telling where, full of germs, little blip blip machines going off all over the place, people I don't know from Adam coming in sticking their finger up my ass and all that. You think I'm gone let myself in for that? Why hell no, why should I get stuck dying for eight or ten years. You don't really know how it is, son, I told him.

But, why hell, I remember when I was sixteen like it was yesterday. Time has a way. But I just up and decided that I'm the one that ought to say how long, not some army of so-called doctors and nurses so overbooked and overstocked and, and so money hungry you have to sit on some sofa in some waiting room for half a day so they can get somebody to come get you and sit you in some little back room for thirty minutes and you sit there on some little hard-ass table looking at certificates and then they come rushing in and look in your ear and rush out and then get some teenager to come in and write a bunch of crap down on a clipboard, so what I'm going to do in the next few days is dig my own damned grave. That's one reason I'm in North Carolina. First things first. One thing at a time. I'm glad it's about my time to go. This country I been seeing since it was most wilderness and I said to him, I said, "I tell you one thing, son. It's going to hell. H-e-l-l. Hell in a breadbasket. Especially around here. I don't even recognize any of it. Look around at them ugly glass mile-high ugly buildings all over the countryside. Look at that so-called—what is it?" I asked him, "That TechComm thing we drove by coming in here."

"TechComm Commons," he says.

"TechComm Commons, with all them ugly buildings with windows that won't even open in the summertime. Hell, no windows, period. No *windows*. Let's go," I say. "You got a car, ain't you?"

"Yeah, but . . ."

"At least let me get out there and let's get started."

"Right now?"

"I don't see why not. Your daddy's gone. You got a car. We got the time. I got the money honey if you got

138

the time. Leave the boys a note and tell them you taking me around to some of my old stomping grounds.

"First thing we do is find some shovels and a pick. Then, after that, we go down to the corner of Third and James at the railroad tracks and get some help." There's where, as long as I can remember, you could pick up niggers looking for work.

Bill

I got this eye that look off to one side. It's got more and more that way the longer I live, and I lived a pretty good while. People I don't even know draw back and say, "What the *hell* you looking at me for?" I say, "It just *look* like I looking at you." See, my eyes is splayed off in different directions—I don't see with the one you think's looking at you. Except sometimes I do see with that one, but I don't understand how it work myself.

I come from my daughter's, down the tracks, to see I can get a little work, and I'm standing around with Melvin, Duck, and Jo-Jo, and two I ain't seen before, when this car pulls up and stops. There's a boy driving, and this old man in the passenger seat. About time they stop, the old man say something to the boy, the boy rolls down his window, and the old man hollers, "Work!" and the boy jumps—scared him.

Jo-Jo walked over to the window and bent down, and listen, and then he come back and say, "Not me."

"What?" I say. They still sitting there looking. The little old man yell again, "Work!"

"Digging a grave," say Jo-Jo.

I walk over to the car. The boy he look spoiled, the old man kind of dried up. "What you paying?" I ask.

"Two dollars an hour," say the old man.

"Shoot, man. That ain't nothing."

"Hell," the old man says, "there'll be three of us doing work for two. You'll get a lot of time off. And there's a bonus."

"Three-fifty," I said.

"I'll give you three."

"I'll do it for three twenty-five."

"Get in."

I get in, and ask the old man, "What kind of bonus?"

"You'll see," he says.

"What kind of grave? Cow or something?"

"Nope."

"What you burying?"

"You ask a lot of questions. Me."

"Me what?—burying *you*? Oh. That's what you gone do. You ain't feeling too good?" I said.

"No, I ain't. What's your name?"

"Bill." Old white man figure he got him a nigger now.

At the graveyard, the old man—well, hell, he ain't too much older than me—lays out the grave. He's got a couple of picks, shovel, even a posthole shovel. And he was real particular about how he laid it out.

140

"My daughter says I'm senile," he say.

I'm standing there leaning on a shovel.

"She says it when she don't think I can hear her. Hell, I can hear a cricket fart in a fast-moving train."

I couldn't exactly figure what was going on, cause then he said he had this story about a dog. I wondered if maybe he was gone bury a dog out there. It's been done. Specially in fresh graves, where the diggin's easy. "What about that dog?" I ask him. He was sitting on this rock wall.

"Just a story."

"That's what I was asking about."

"I used to raise dogs from the dead." Then he tell this story about a man bring this little dog back to life with that mouth-to-mouth. Funny story. Then he says, "Dig." Then he says, "What the hell you looking at me like that for?"

I explain about my eye. My eye goes a long way toward explaining why I ain't ever made no money.

8

Grove

*T*HIS NIGGER—BILL—TURNED OUT TO BE A GOOD worker. But it was taking too long, and so we drove over and got a buddy of Bill's and left them to finish up. Paid them good. Me and the boy, Morgan, had to get back so things wouldn't look fishy.

The boy done all right. Promised to keep his mouth shut. Nothing happens, and I can get me a coffin made, then tomorrow night is the night.

Looks like poor old Glenn will be out there, too—in the graveyard. Poor old Glenn spent his last ten years inside the house. I don't know how he done it.

I never had nothing against Glenn. I feel sorry for that wife having to put up with them sisters, so forth and so on, but at least she didn't have to put up with his mama and papa for too long. Whew.

It would have been nice if somebody could have got a holt to that farm back when, and kept it up.

Me and the boy got back from digging before Tate and Faison got back from the homeplace. The boy changed his shoes. Since I was supervising, mine were mostly clean. He showed me some more stuff about his computer. I made out like I understood. Four-Eyes, my daughter's husband, has got a computer. Beyond me. I asked the boy how he felt about his granddaddy. He said he'd never known him to be anything but sick. Shame.

I turned on a ball game in the living room and the boy went on with his computing.

When Faison and Tate come in they were both a little shook up. It was up in the air who was going to get the homeplace, looked like. Tate wanted to talk to—let's see—it would be his stepsister, but Faison wanted to hold off. They got to figure who gets the land, see.

That used to be a nice piece of land. I remember it well. Evelyn wanted to get off it and into town for some reason. Poor Evelyn.

Me and the boy went to the grocery store. I got us some corn on the cob, ham, and cabbage. Tate set up a little card table and a white tablecloth in his living room there and we all pulled up chairs. I was tired, and hurting some. It had been a good, long day.

"You don't like cabbage, boy?" I says.

"No."

"No sir," said Tate.

"I beat Junior's ass for not saying 'sir,' " says Faison.

"We never knew not to say it," I said. Then I says to Morgan, I says, "If you gone be able to out-fart me, you got to eat some cabbage."

He looked at his daddy. "Out-fart you? I didn't know we were going to have a contest."

"I'm sleeping in your room, ain't I?"

"I don't know. I—"

"You'll be sleeping in my room," said Tate. "I'm going to sleep out here on the couch. It's a foldout."

So I'm sitting there at a little table with a white tablecloth eating cabbage and ham with the family. Sitting with these boys I tried to half-raise—done grown, boys of their own. Well, one boy. Everybody else dead or gone. I had to decide what I was going to do. Shoot myself and get somebody to bury me? Wait and die? Run off? I was tired of hurting every afternoon. I didn't want to go through something like Glenn went through.

"You boys ever see Albert and them, anymore?" I said. "What's his name, over in Draughn?"

"Once in a while," said Tate. "Not much."

"Least they got a little piece of land," said Faison.

"Well, it's a damn shame you boys could lose the farm. But listen to what I'm fixing to say. You got your health. Think about that—and you both got a job."

"The land stuff should be settled by Friday," says Faison, "but I'm going fishing anyway, come hell or high water."

He said he was going down to McGarren Island, down there among some of them Outer Banks, where I used to fly to. Wanted to know didn't I want to go.

I had to tend to my business. One way or the other. I told him we'd see.

I suggested we get out the whiskey and drink a toast to the old man. We did, with the boy looking like he won't sure what was going on, and damn if Tate didn't start to crying. Hell, they don't have to be good to you for you to miss them. I told him to go ahead, it was okay, and things were a little shaky until we had another round or two and the boy got to giggling—course he won't drinking—about something I said, hell, I don't remember what, and the next thing I knew I was telling them all about the time back in '36 when I got that load of pure alcohol on Bud Dumby's first run. Now that was the time. Pure alcohol and I didn't know it. I thought it was whiskey. But this was pure alcohol, stole from the government.

Well, what it was, I pulled in up there at Midway, this side of Savannah. I always stopped there and got a bite to eat. Knew the people well, you know, and they made some of the best biscuits in there I ever eat, and if they didn't have them hot when you got in there they'd just slip them in the oven, see. And so I pulled up to the gas tank, and I said to the boy was with me on that trip, just a kid, Bud Dumby—you try to say it: Bud Dumby. We ended up calling him Dud. I says to him, I said, "Dud, ten to one our biscuits will be hot." They were, too.

This guy in there told me the location of my pickup in New York, and said it would all be in fifty-gallon drums and five-gallon cans. Nothing unusual about that. So we drove on through Washington and into New York.

We got up there, to the spot, and me and Dud was

sitting there and it was almost dark and I seen this fellow come up out of the under park—you know, where they've got them trains all under New York. And when he come up out of there he had on a overcoat. I said, "There's the man, right yonder." And sure enough it was. He walked on over to us, and he said, "Do you know anything about Boston Post Road?" And I said, "Yes, that's part of one of my runs."

"Well," he said, "we'll go out and hit the Boston Post Road. I'll lead you to the place." This driver comes up in a big black car and picks him up. I said to myself, This is unusual. But I didn't want Dud to know. This was his first run and all.

We finally pulled in behind that black car at Andy Reece's truck stop and the guy in the overcoat was already out of his car. Another man in a overcoat come up from somewhere and said, "Back it right down side the station here." I was thinking to myself that if I saw we were about to get shot—for the truck, you know— we might have to make a run for it. It was a little tense there. This is when I seen this guy standing over here and another one over here, round there was another one—all in overcoats with their hands in their pockets. This was not at all what I'd been used to, you know what I mean.

Did I say this was Dud's first run? Well, it was. And when I said, "Dud, something's fishy here. We might have to make a run for it," well, Dud started shaking. Just a shaking. I was thinking hard as I could the way to make a break for it—probably on foot, or once we got inside, out the bathroom window, or somehow, and I looked at him sitting there in the cab, and his knees were hitting together, his hands were shaking, and damned if his head won't jerking around and I'm thinking this is just what I don't need. This was his first run, young boy in the bootlegging business—his wife and kid had seen him off, kissed him and everything—and he looked like he was gone faint. So I said, "Son, you think you can hold still?" and he said, "No sir, I don't think I can."

The first guy walked over next to the step-up and yells up to me, "Let's go in the restaurant and get us a steak." Well, he might as well hit me between the eyes with a hammer. This kind of stuff just never happened.

"Bring the boy, too," he says.

Right here is where Dud starts in with this low moan. I say, "Let's go, Dud, I don't think we have no choice," and he goes, "Ahhhhh ahhhhh."

We get inside and sit down in a booth. Dud's shaking like something's got a hold of him. Louise, the waitress—I knew her—drops a wet rag in front of him and says, "Push that around a minute, honey. I'll be right back."

He puts his hand on the rag, looks up at her walking away, and he's as white as a sheet, and his head falls right over onto that wet rag. Out. Then in a few seconds his head comes back up. He looks at the man in the overcoat. His head goes over again.

"What the *hell* is wrong with him?" the man asks me. He's across the table from us.

"I don't know," I say. "I guess he fainted."

A couple of people have noticed.

Dud's head comes back up. He looks at me, desperate-like. See, when your head falls over, the blood to your brain brings you back around. If your head's propped up, you stay out.

"Hold on a minute, Dud," I said. But he's gone again. If that rag hadn't been there he'd a hurt hisself, sure.

A *lot* of people have noticed by now.

Dud is up again.

"Next time," says the man, "prop his head up so he'll stay out, goddammit. This is ridiculous." Something like that.

Dud straightens up. Starts back down. I catch him and sort of prop his head back in the corner of the booth and finish wiping off the table.

Louise comes with her order pad out, looks at Dud, leaning back, out, and she says, "What'll it be?"

"Steaks," says the man.

"Is he okay?" she says to me.

"Yeah. He's napping."

"What kind of steaks?"

"T-bone."

"How you want them done?"

"Rare for me," says the man.

"Medium," I say. "And he likes his well-done."

When Louise left the man whispers to me pretty direct and sincere, you know what I mean, he whispers, "This is making a goddamn scene. We don't need a goddamn scene, Grove. Wake the boy up, get him outside and around back. My boys will watch him."

I didn't think that was a very good idea. This man hadn't even told me his name yet. "Let's get him some horseradish to nibble on," I said. "That'll keep him awake and, you know, looking normal. I think that'll cause less trouble than taking him around back. This is his first run." Hell, I didn't know if horseradish would work. But I just walked back in the kitchen and got some.

It worked. Brought him out of the fainting, but not the shaking. The steaks came and we ate them—except Dud didn't eat much—and by that time the truck was back, loaded, with what turned out to be pure alcohol, not whiskey. These boys had stole it from the U.S. government and if I'd got caught, I'd still be in jail.

We brought it all the way back down to Darien, Georgia. Dud stopped shaking somewhere in Tennessee.

It all worked out fine. Yeah, it worked out fine. We unloaded and me and Dud washed her down. And in the end, as per normal, I got two dollars a mile for the whole trip. And this was in 1936.

Morgan

Uncle Faison left after this long story Uncle Grove told. Man he's been through a lot. He's a good story-teller. He makes these really old stories seem like they just happened—right outside somewhere. But he's a lit-tle crazy, too. I can see why Uncle Faison ran away to go live with him.

Dad was talking on the phone to the funeral home,

and then somebody else, then to this lawyer. Uncle Grove was watching "60 Minutes." This grave-digging stuff had to be some kind of joke or something. But I figured he could do whatever he wanted to. The footstone had his name on it. He said he mailed it to Dad and Uncle Faison. I don't know what he's going to do, but I hadn't told because I promised him I wouldn't. We like shook on it.

I cleaned up the dishes and stuff in the kitchen. I didn't know what to put the cabbage in. I put it in this bowl and put a little plate on top for a cover. I loaded the dishwasher, put in the detergent, and when I came back in Dad was off the phone and Uncle Grove was talking about bird hunting—all this stuff about watching a dog work and all. Then he said he wanted to tell me about this gun I was going to get. Then he went into this stuff about somebody named Ross shooting a hole in the wall with it one time. Then he said, "We let that nigger have it to—"

I flashed. He said it before and I hadn't said anything about it. "They are not 'niggers.' They are people," I said. "They are African-Americans."

"I call them niggers," he said. And he goes right ahead. He wouldn't pay any attention if he didn't want to. Sometimes he would look right at me and call me by name and all this, and then next time around if I like said something he didn't want to hear, he'd ignore me.

He was telling about somebody tearing up a liquor still close to their house when he was a little boy. He explained where it was. He explains by pointing to where this place was, then runs his finger along an imaginary road and points, like there's a little map right there in front of you. He'll say, Our house set back here, and here's the old road coming, turned down here, and went around here, come right back in down here by the old barn. Right across old man Fernigan's place and right over there is the still. He calls this man a "nigger" but Dad doesn't say a thing. His name was Shaw and Uncle Grove said he could "call out weights. Ten eggs is a pound; pound of wheat flour is a quart." Such as that. He said he used to take a fertilizer sack and wash it, clean it good, cut holes in it, and like that's what his children used for clothes.

Grove

And we give that nigger that gun. I think he had six shells. And he didn't go down the barn path. He walked right straight across the field. And he wadn't gone ten minutes when we heard that shooting over there. If he'd had that rifle or buckshot, he'd killed everyone of them.

And he come back in the night, with the shotgun, right when we were eating supper. You always worked till dark. Then you eat after dark. He put the gun back up over the door and sat down right there at the door, kind of listening out the door and he told us the whole story about how he got in there close and shot one in the chest with bird shot and then backed out of there, a tree at a time, shooting.

And he had two trickles of dried blood down the side of his head.

When we finished eating, Papa got up, walked over and more or less inspected his head, then had him sit down at the table, put his hands down by his side, and rest his head on a rolled-up coat.

Papa made us all sit along by the wall. Oh, I can see it now. That light from the oil lamps on the wall and the one Papa had Mama to hold right up over Shaw's head.

And Papa pared that skin with his pocket knife and picked out two buckshot, one just above his ear and one right back here. Picked them out. Yeah, it wadn't completely gone, you know what I mean. Just under the skin, see. They were shot from too far off to go on through that skull of his, and the rest of the shot hit that gun stock. There was just two shots hit him, and I believe there was one in his hand. Three hit him altogether. The one in his hand went in too deep to mess with. And I can see him at that table right now as clear as if it was yesterday.

So, I said to Junior—to Morgan, I mean—that's the gun you're gone get because these boys will get it when I go my way and you're the next one in line. It's a good old gun—a lot of history around it.

The boy was all agitated about what people called each other back then. That's what they get in the public schools. I told him about after I got grown coming across this same Shaw when he was a old man, just as white-headed as a ball of cotton, and I was with Clar-

ence Turner and Clarence said, "Mr. Shaw, you know
who this is?" and he looked at me, and Clarence said,
"It's Grove McCord, Uncle Tad's boy," and I want you
to know that old nigger hugged me, and cried like I
was one of his own. He sure did. Aw, we were good to
each other back in those days. Nothing but good to each
other. Now, back when they had the slaves, I can't say
nothing about that. But I don't care what they say, you
got your niggers, and you got your poor white trash,
and then, too, you got people with good hearts, all
colors, and people like me, who try anyway. And you
know, whatever you leave behind is your history, and it
better be good, because you're history longer than
you're fact.

Faison

I drove up to the funeral home to see what the hell
was going on about the autopsies. If they didn't have
them right away then it wouldn't do no good.

It all fell apart.

I know Mr. Simmons, the main man up at the funeral
home, so I figured he'd let me know about any investigation, if one had been started. Drew had laid the
groundwork on the thing and I didn't want to bug him
anymore. For all I knew, they had already done the

autopsies, and knew which one died first, which I had to find out so as to, you know, get the lay of the land—as you might say.

When I got up there, Mr. Simmons said a couple of men were in with the bodies. I waited. When they come out I introduced myself and all that and told them I was concerned, what could they tell me. They said they were looking for some kind of probable cause of foul play, or something like that.

We're standing in the hall outside the door to the room where the bodies are, and all of a sudden with her coattails all flying out behind her, who comes sashaying up but—yeah, right—Faye.

"What's going on, Faison?" she says to me, like these guys weren't even standing there. And she had fire in her eyes like . . . like a mad dog.

"I don't know," I said, telling the honest truth.

These two men start to walk off.

"Just a minute," she says, and they stop.

She introduces herself to these guys, sticks out her hand, and her voice is shaking. "Please don't go anywhere," she says to them, then she turns on me. "I know what you're doing, Faison Bales, and you can call the whole thing off. There will be no autopsy—over my dead body there will be an autopsy of my mother. Do you understand what I'm saying?"

So I say as calm as I can, "There may have been some foul play involved." I mean, I figure I got to hold the line now.

"No there wasn't," she spits out. "I checked that girl out thoroughly before I hired her. I did all that and I've talked to her since last night. Have you?"

154

"Well, no," I said. "I didn't want to interrupt no investigation."

And then, boy, did she do one on me. She was literally shaking all over and she told those guys—I don't know, I guess it was the coroner and an investigator or somebody—that if there was an autopsy on her mama she would sue the city of Summerlin into the next century and back, and then she hopped on me about being a land-grabbing no good son of a bitch, low-country worm something.

WHOA, I said, you goddamned spruced-up, slick, god-damned I don't know what-all and I told her she wasn't going to get any of my family's land because it won't right for her to come in out of nowhere— especially *Charlotte*—and get it all.

And she said that I didn't have no choice and if I had known the first thing about the law, or if I'd had the decency to come to her, then I wouldn't be *sneaking around* in the funeral home trying to find out who died first.

Now that did kind of run all over me. I felt like choking her. And here is where she laid some very bad or very good news on me. I haven't taken it in, yet. I'll have to talk to our lawyer who ought to have known about this if it's true, but he didn't. This is it: in North Carolina, she said, if two people, like a husband and wife, die within twenty-four hours of each other, then by *law*, get this now, by *law*, they died at the *same time*. Some kind of simultaneous something something. She was spitting that stuff out right and left.

I kept my hands in my pockets. If she had been a

man, I'd had him in every corner of that place at one time.

So, anyway, what it all comes down to is that me and Tate don't get the whole place, but it means by god we don't end up empty-handed either.

You would not believe the way that woman looked at me. But I know good and well she would have done the same thing in my shoes. Anybody would.

I mean, look. Now, listen. When I grew up on that place, I was fresh out of a mama, and I worked hard in them fields. My old man was gone all week, every week, and in the late summertimes when Aunt Bette and Aunt Ansie were babying around with Tate on the front porch or some such, I was cropping sand lugs—tobacco. You ever cropped any tobacco? Try it. One day. See how it is. There's not any work that I know about that will touch it as far as worseness is concerned. Multiply that by all the days I did it all day long.

See, *I'm* the one got the shit jobs. Tate was a precious little thing. They protected him. I got the shit jobs. The whole time I was growing up, from the time I was seven on, while my mama was gone and my daddy was away working, and then from twelve to sixteen, while Ma Laura was there giving me a hard time, that farm, friend, that farm got to be my mama and daddy, my brother and sister, and my boss, and I knew every damned inch of it like the back of my hand, and there won't no job on that farm, hard job, that I didn't do, because you see, my granddaddy was getting too old, and my daddy was gone, so I was what you call the man of the place. All the while, my buddies played on baseball teams in the summer and went to Boy Scout camp and all this while I'm doing grub work on that farm, and after I left it all started going downhill. And I by god deserve a piece of it now that it's been more or less freed up. The truth is I deserve it all. That's the truth of the matter. But now who do I share it with? A female Charlotte lawyer and my baby brother.

And who do I leave my part to when I'm dead and gone?

At least I'm glad that while he was alive, Junior didn't have to go through all I went through. I'm glad I was around for him, and June Lee was, too, and I'm glad he got to play ball up to his last year of Little League.

Tate

This morning Uncle Grove had a bad case of diarrhea, and I had to help him clean up. He kept apologizing, and was very embarrassed. I'm glad Morgan was still in bed.

Daddy was on my mind, and something had happened at the funeral home that I haven't heard the straight of. Aunt Ansie called me about it last night. Mr. Simmons had called her. Faison and Faye got into it up there.

I wanted to ride out to the airfield to show Uncle Grove the airplane. He said he felt okay, so we went.

It was cool and clear out there and the sun was in just the tops of the trees. The grass had almost filled out. Uncle Grove wanted to come out in the morning because he says he starts hurting in the afternoon. He's not a complainer so I know it must be something fairly serious. He won't go to the doctor or take any medicine at all, not even aspirin, so I'm going to slip aspirin in his coffee and tea this week, and see if that makes a difference.

At the airfield, Daddy was still on my mind of course. Maybe if I'd been with him just before he died, he might have said he was sorry he hadn't spent more time with us when we were little, said something about all that. Maybe I could have set him up in bed and bathed his back, or something—something that I could remember. I know I should have talked things over with him at some point, but it always seemed like a later time would be best.

Guilt is normal. And there are grieving stages to accept and not fight. I'll be okay if I don't fight it. Faison will fight showing any emotion. I'm not going to.

"Let me get up in there," said Uncle Grove, at the airplane.

"Sure. Just reach up there and—"

"I know how to get in," he says. "Hell, I got in one almost every day for twelve years. Son of a gun if it don't smell the same. It *smells* the same. No better smell in the world," he says. "Hardly."

He settled into the pilot's seat up front. "Why hell," he says, "let's go for a spin."

I'd flown the airplane from the backseat, so I said okay. "Do you want me to talk you through?" I asked him.

"No. Just keep an eye on me. Follow me through on the controls in case I forget something."

I got on the controls. He brought her to life and taxied out to the end of the strip.

"Hell, this is like I was flying yesterday," he said. "We got a, what's this, hundred and fifty drop on the left mag, two hundred on the right. Let's see, carb heat, little drop, run her up, looks good. Re*lease* the brakes. Hold on back there, boy—here we go!"

I held to the controls, lightly. The stick came back between my legs—he was doing a short-field takeoff. We were airborne. He pushed the stick forward as soon as we were in the air, lowering the nose about right. He was steady, holding about eighty miles an hour on the climb out. A little hot, but fine. He was lax on rudder but he was doing it, doing it all.

"She flies good," he said, over his shoulder, back to me.

Lamar Benfield

I been working for Claremont Funeral Home and Marbleworks for about two months now. I was looking for outside work that would build up my muscles. Toting tombstones is perfect, and we do a little shovel work along with the backhoe. Good hours, don't have to work in the rain.

We were supposed to dig out seven-two-A—me and Isaac—one of a double plot, out at the big church graveyard just this side of Listre, and then do seven-two-B right after that funeral so they could do another funeral right then, or the next day—I don't know which. It was a double death, car accident or some such I guess and somebody wanted a pink tombstone, but there had been a mix-up about that because, one thing, a footstone was already there. But listen to the other thing. Me and Isaac got over there to the spot and found ourselves looking at the grave *already dug*.

We double-checked everything. We had the plot map and all.

"Looks like they mussa got somebody else to do it," says Isaac.

"Yeah," I said. "Let's go to Big Al's. We got time for a game of pool."

We've had the same thing happen twice before. They give the same job to two different teams.

We had time for four games. I won all four.

Uncle Grove and I were sitting in the living room at Dad's. He'd called me away from a game of Tetris. Dad was taking a call from the funeral home.

"Listen," Uncle Grove says, and he motioned me over closer. "I told Tate I was staying with Faison, and Faison thinks I'll be over here. All you got to do is come out there in the morning at sunup and fill in the grave and do a funeral. I want it at sunup, and then I want you to call my hometown paper in Arkansas and tell them. It's the *Cutler Morning Edition*. Write that down."

I got out my billfold, pulled out a piece of paper, and wrote. It was some kind of joke, so I figured I'd go along with it. He was paying me good.

"Don't back out on me, you hear," he said.

"I won't," I said. "What are you going to do after you do the trick?"

He said he was going to take a vacation then head on back home and surprise everybody. Then he started in with all these other details about how he was leaving some money at the grave for me and Bill, that we'd have to nail in the nails and drop the coffin down with two ropes, pile on the dirt, read the Twenty-third something—Psalms. Something in the Bible. He said a note to his wife would be in his coat pocket. All this stuff like you'd see on TV almost. I wrote it all down and had just stuck it in my billfold when Dad came back in.

Uncle Grove kept on talking. "Now you get yourself

married sometime after you're twenty-seven and have a little boy and give him that gun when you find yourself slowing down. I tell you something. I met Huey Smith when he was twenty-seven and I was seven, and then I remember being forty-seven and I realized I myself was twenty years older than *he'd* been when I thought he was a old man at twenty-seven and I knew then that when I was twenty years older than he was right then, then I'd be a very old man. And I'm already older than that and if Huey Smith was alive he'd be, oh let's see, a hundred and two, no, twelve. Now ain't that something? And they think I'm crazy,'' he said to Dad.

I think he might be. Something's wrong with him.

Grove

I was at the gravesite. It was after dark. Tate and Faison were doing legal shenanigans somewhere. Each one thought I was at the othern's house.

It had been seeming like I was almost through with living for a long time. It seemed like if I didn't handle all the carrying-ons about dying then I'd go to my grave unfinished. In other words, I myself, Grove McCord, wouldn't have finished it all, and it would haunt me the whole time I was history, which would be a long, long time—forever as a matter of fact. I had to finish it. I had to be the one. I couldn't leave it up to anybody else. I'd been worrying about digging my own grave in this graveyard for a long time, and now all I had to do more or less was go through all the motions, and this was my chance, away from Tina and Bobbie and Four-Eyes.

It was a unusually warm night, but so early in the spring that the mosquitoes won't all that bad yet. The man delivered the box like he was supposed to, after dark.

"You the one wants this?" he says.

"I'm the one."

"Where you want it?"

"Just put it on the ground there. What I owe you?"

"Hundred and twenty-five."

"You said a hundred on the phone."

"Twenty-five for the delivery."

"You said one hundred dollars delivered."

"Look, I got to make a living, you know? The box costs me eighty dollars to make—in materials. It's like a cabinet. That ain't but a twenty-percent markup, not including labor. And I'm delivering. I could be making another box while I'm delivering this one."

I managed to sit down on the box. He caught my arm as I started down. Young fellow.

"Did you put a hook and latch inside?" I asked.

"I did. What's that for? Some kind of joke?"

"Yeah. It is."

"Well, I got to get my money and go. This whole thing is pretty strange."

I pulled out my roll of bills, pulled off six twenties. The moon was bright enough to see by. I looked for a five. "That honeysuckle smells good, don't it. Or whatever it is." I found a five. "There's your damn hundred and twenty-five, but you either lied to me or your mouth and your mind ain't working together." Hell, maybe I was the one got it wrong. "Sit down on this box a minute. I want to tell you something, son."

He stood there, then sat.

"How old are you?" I asked him.

"Thirty-two."

"Let me tell you something. I never had a son."

"Oh."

"Something else, I knew a man when he was twenty-seven years old and I thought he was a old man. You know how old he is now?"

"No, I don't."

"He's dead. Something else." Then I told him about my papa. When Papa died, people come in from Bethel, Summerlin, from all around, and I want you to know they plowed out the whole farm in one day. And another time we had a barn burn down. Lost all our harnesses, six bales of cotton. People came, brought lumber on a Friday morning, laid out the lumber, and by Saturday noon, that barn was built back. Nobody charged nothing. Why—and here I had to laugh, I guess, sort of a laugh—Why son, I said, people don't want to even *look* at you no more. And if they do, they look at you like they *hate* you. People do.

He said he had to go, and stood up.

I went on anyway about how across the yard down to the barn we had all these apple trees. June apples, horse apples, good horse apples. Made cider. Mule apples. Three pear trees. And let's see, between the house and the barn was one, two, three, four, five, six, seven—seven big white oaks. The sun didn't hit the yard except for oh, ten-thirty to one-thirty in the summertime. There were lilies there that I guarantee you still come up today.

He walked on over toward his truck. "Yeah, well," he said, "good luck with that coffin. It's well made." He slammed the door, cranked the truck, and drove off.

Bill

Me and Duck end up at the CFM not all that far from the graveyard me and Melvin been digging a grave in for that old man. So I said, "Duck, let's go over there to the back side of the graveyard and I'll show you a nice piece of work."

There was a bright moon and all, so we head on over. We get close by and I say, "Hush, hush. There's somebody over there. Shhhhh. Come on." So we creeped up on somebody kneeling down—over there by that very grave I was bringing Duck to see, kneeling down like he was praying. We creeped up into the corner of that little rock wall and we was right at him.

"And Papa," he say. "Papa, Papa. I'm coming to join you. It's the only thing left to do. I'm shitting down my leg every few days now. People have to clean me up. There ain't nowhere else to go. We got the whole place plowed out after you died. And well . . . I made friends wherever I went. Some good. Some not so good.''

All this stuff. I recognized the voice, clear. The same old white man, name of Grove. His head was in his hands. He was kneeling beside a box, a *coffin*. He raised a foot, slow, started getting up, stumble a little bit, finally got up straight. "Ah, lord," he say. Duck, he being quiet and still. The old man push the box over to a spot beside the grave. Pushed with his foot. We watch him, you know. It all feels a little bit like it's on the TV. He pick up two long lengths of rope laying across a tombstone, drop one at each end of the coffin, open the coffin lid, stand there looking into the box. This was getting a little bit spooky. Then. Then he pulled out a *pistol* from his back pocket and drapped down to his knees, and then turned this way and that and finally got sitiated, sitting there in this open coffin. I said to myself, I'm dreaming, sure. Then he laid down on it, reached up, but he couldn't reach the lid. So he finally got back up and pulled the lid down agin his shoulder, then laid down, close the lid. Just like that. He close the lid. I say to Duck, I say, "I'm coming to work here in a morning, getting fifty bucks to bury the old son of a bitch. And that's a fact.''

We could hear something what sound like a screen-door latch be handled inside there. Then it clicked solid. Then there was a knocking sound against the wood. I look at Duck. Duck look at me, raise his eyebrows, look kind of sleepy, and he whisper, "I just got the idea we ought to be getting out of here. Somebody gone lay this on *us*."

It was like he was knocking around in there with a monkey wrench, and all on a sudden we hear this muffle-up explosion, this bang, in the coffin, and these sparks flash off this great big tombstone, and Duck is up and running, and just as fast he's laying on the ground moaning, holding his leg. He done hit this knee-high tombstone, and I don't know whether to laugh or cry.

I helped him up and we get on back over to the 7-Eleven, but it look like over there they didn't hear the shot, it being in the coffin and all that, so we hang around a minute, buy one more bottle of Mad Dog, and I decide to go back and take a look, see what be the case, now. Find out if anybody else heard and maybe come up on the old man. I was curious. Duck, he didn't want to go, but I had the bottle so he finally say okay.

We get back over there, and there that coffin still sitting just the same, six or eight feet from that open grave. It's one of them old-timey pine boxes. Lord, I seen many a one. And sure 'nough, there's a hole blasted in it about shoulder high.

"This crazy, man," says Duck.

"What we gone do?" I say.

"Get out of here."

"Let's knock on the door."

"Naw, man." And this all on the sudden strike Duck as funny and so he start kind of laughing. See, we don't know whether he dead or not but we too high to care too much about anything, so Duck kind of walk on up there between the grave and the coffin and he look all around—he's got right brave, see—and he squat down and knock on the door.

"We could get shot," I say.

"This a good a place as any," he say.

We hear the latch getting played with, then the door *fly* open and there's a pistol pointed right between Duck's eyes and he's trying to stand up and walk backwards at the same time when he disappear from the earth into that open grave.

"Mr. Grove!" I say. "Don't shoot. It's just old Bill."

"I'm trying to take a nap," he say.

"It's just me, Bill," I say. "And my man just fell in your grave," and then I hear Duck moaning down in there. Then he got stood up, and his head was at the top of the grave, so I got him out, but it won't easy.

I asked the old man what in the hell he was doing and he said he had a change of heart and decided to just take a nap, and would we help him find a place to spend the night. Truth is, he has some stuck valves. His wheels has lost some spokes.

There's a Motel 6 over behind the CFM—he had some money I knew—so we walk along to over there and he talked about all kinds of wonderments: apple trees and girlfriends and cancer. Duck, he wadn't in too good a shape. He'd got kind of beat up out in the graveyard.

We got the old man checked in a room, him still a-talking. Duck told him they'd left the light on for him. He wouldn't drink no wine with us, so we left and headed on home. I needed to get some sleep myself. The boy was going to pick me up at sunup to bury the box and fill in the grave.

Sometimes I wonder about the peoples I get work with.

June Lee

I let Faison spend the night with me. He's been through a lot. He was pretty wrung out and when we finally went to bed he reached over and touched me on the shoulder and I was as hungry for him as anything I can ever remember. He hadn't said much since he'd got here. He hadn't needed to, I guess. His daddy died and it don't matter too much that they weren't all that close.

I told him, I said, Faison, Faison this is the time when you need somebody. There is some things you can't just carry around on your own. You think you can. But you can't. You need somebody to listen, and all the time we was together, Faison, one of us was strong when the other was broke down, and now when something goes bad, we ain't neither one got nobody to be there. Don't you see you need somebody, Faison?

The bad time when Junior died in the wreck, we didn't either one have nobody then. I wanted his real name, John Moody, Jr., on his tombstone, and Faison wanted his own name with the Junior on there. That tore us apart right when we needed each other more than at any other time in our lives.

Faison was mostly quiet just about the whole time he was here—but I guess he had seen that he needed somebody, since he came over.

I fixed him some eggs and bacon next morning and he went to work. They suddenly got more work than they can handle. Looks like everybody wants to move their house now. But he says he's going fishing anyway. I'm glad. He needs a break. And if he gets rich out of the homeplace being sold, I might believe it, but I won't believe it until I see the green in his hand.

Faye

I was tired. Couldn't sleep. I was remembering Mother's face, her gestures, her smile, from times before she'd married Glenn Bales. The old days. But of course the travesty of Faison's attempts at an autopsy had intruded on everything, everything decent. What a poor excuse for a human being.

I finally got up at about four-thirty, drank some coffee, and decided that when daylight came I'd drive out to the gravesite. I had an uneasy feeling about it. I'd never been out there and couldn't remember how it was all supposed to be set up exactly. Mrs. Fuller talked about it all the time. Something had been said about a pink footstone. I was glad it had all been taken care of, but then, too, I was curious.

I had a set of written directions to Mother's gravesite, and when I got to the graveyard, I saw two men filling in a grave. I rechecked my directions because it seemed these two men were very near Mother's gravesite. As I approached I saw the BALES tombstone. Mother's grave was to be the one on the right. I realized that two men were filling in *my mother's grave! Morgan?—Tate's son?*—and, and a very old black man.

I walked across the wet grass. "What are you doing?" I said. "Aren't you Morgan?"

"Why?" he says, stepping back, like he's been caught at something.

"We just had a little funeral," said the old man, who looked in dire need of a change of clothes.

"A funeral? Who? This was—did you bury my *mother*?"

Morgan, I knew it was Morgan, just stood there, with that guilty look. I think he's about fourteen.

"No," said the man. "We might have bury somebody's daddy, but we ain't bury nobody's mama."

"Do you realize this is my mother's grave?"

"Not right now I don't think it is," he said.

"Oh my god." I brought my hands to my face. I turned and started walking away. This was some kind of ultimate humiliation. To think that I would have to share one blade of grass from that farm with anybody in that godforsaken family. I stumbled. I had never felt such exhaustion. I dropped to the ground, and sat, to try to turn loose—for a minute—the whole mess that Mother had gotten into when she married that Glenn

Bales, with those boys, and those aunts, and all these horrible country people.

WRBR

We interrupt for a local news bulletin. A visitor to Summerlin, Grove McCord, of Cutler, Arkansas, apparently buried himself alive last night in the Listre Baptist Church cemetery right here just outside Listre, North Carolina. A suicide note was found but has not been released by the sheriff's department. Two men are being held as accomplices. One is a vagrant named William Turpentine and the other is a minor whose name was not released. The suicide motive was apparently related to the deaths from natural causes of Mr. McCord's relatives, Mr. and Mrs. Glenn Bales, of Listre. Our own Tim Venable is headed to the scene and we'll keep you updated . . . Stand by. I've been handed a note here that says . . . a bullet hole has been found in McCord's coffin there at the site. Speculation now is that the victim may have been shot after he was dead and then taken to another location away from the cemetery. We'll definitely keep you posted as events unfold. Now, back to the music. Here are Summerlin's own Noble Defenders of the Word.

Wilma Fuller

Betty Donaldson had just called me with all the news when Harold walked in. I said, "Harold, where have you been?"

"Out to the graveyard."

"Then you know," I said.

"I seen it with my own eyes."

"Grove McCord is back in town," I said, "and he committed suicide and him and Miss Laura *and* Mr. Glenn almost ended up buried in the same grave together. It's the worse thing I've ever heard in my life. All that hard feeling and misunderstanding from years and years of bad blood almost dumped into the same hole. Lord, it would be like burying I don't know who-all together."

"I was there," says Harold. "I *been* out there, Wilma. I know what happened. There's a lot of people out there. There's TV people out there." Sometimes Harold gets off the subject.

"They said Grove shot himself up in the coffin," I said, "and got buried alive, and then Faye walked up on it, and somebody shot a gun."

"No. No, what happened was—"

"They said some people think he might *still* be alive in there."

"Wilma. Will you be quiet a minute? He ain't alive in there. He won't even in there at all."

"Really?" That was news. "Who said so?"

"Wilma, do you know where I just came from?"

"The graveyard." What kind of question was that?

"Yes, the graveyard. *I been out there, Wilma.* I was out there when they dug up the coffin. It was a pine box with just some rocks and dirt in it."

"Oh, my . . . my lord. You mean he *arose*?"

"Wilma. Wilma, he won't ever in the box. They just dug it up. Drew said they was thinking about charging some wino with murder until they found out nobody was dead. Well, except Miss Laura and Mr. Glenn. They're dead. No question about that. And now it looks like Grove had dibs on one of their graves. Somebody is going to have to dig another grave or two. At least one more."

And Harold heads for his chair. He'd missed his nap.

I couldn't believe my ears.

Grove

I was tired and sleepy, but happy. From the cockpit, I saw that old graveyard. Then it was a field of cotton, great big white cotton balls. I'd dust it, I figured. I'd dusted some crops in my time. Back on the power in the dive. Level her out, so you can pull the dust knob just before the plants come under the nose. Great big white cotton plants. Just like riding a bicycle. Like riding a bicycle. I hadn't lost my touch. Line her up, down them rows. Now, power back in.

Some people standing around out there. Cotton pickers maybe. Can't poison them. Give them a little show. Where's that damn fuel gauge? But it wadn't a cotton field. By god, it was my graveyard and . . . I couldn't find the fuel gauge. Where was it?

I come to the decision I had to get on back and try to land the thing.

I was too tired to fly much.

Tate

At Daddy's funeral I felt very, very heavy. I didn't know I'd be so tired.

We'd found Uncle Grove at the airport and got him settled at Faison's. He'd taken my airplane up. I don't know what to do about it all. It was too much to handle at once. And now Morgan has developed some kind of odd loyalty to Uncle Grove, which I'm thankful for, but, hell, it could get dangerous. Uncle Grove has a pistol and won't give it up. But at least Sheriff Swain has dropped all charges against the Turpentine man.

Aunt Bette and Aunt Ansie were so mad at us for taking in Uncle Grove they wouldn't sit on the same row with us at Daddy's funeral, and wouldn't speak to us beforehand or afterwards. They were upset about the farm coming to me, Faison, and Faye. I think they'd figured all along that somehow they were going to get some of it. I'm sure if Daddy had left a will they would have.

That Daddy was gone, vanished from earth, leaving a black space where he once had been—this would settle in on me for a few seconds, lift, and in minutes settle in again.

The newsreel ran in my head. The last time I walked out of that room, I turned at the door and Daddy raised his head a little, lifted his hand and said, "Bring me a newspaper sometime. I'm feeling like reading a little bit."

I remember when I was the height of his waist. I remember holding his hand as we walked into Durham Athletic Park to see the Bulls play baseball. I remember his face from below, as a child looks up—the same way I looked at his head on the pillow in those last years, as if from below.

I remember one time when I was a boy and I rubbed my cheek against the hard bristles on his cheek. I remember thinking, I will never forget this minute.

I remember looking at his belt buckle when he unbuckled it to whip Faison, and later, for a while, me. I remember the burning when he whipped me.

I remember him driving up in the dust on Friday afternoons, over and over, and then on Sundays—after we'd all gone to church together—driving away in the dust, while I stood and watched until Aunt Bette or Aunt Ansie called me.

And then later when Daddy worked closer to home,

he'd come in tired and go to sleep in his chair. Ma Laura would make Faison and me leave him alone. His head would be back, his mouth open.

Behind a dark, black wall stood all that could have been if he hadn't had to work all the time. An afternoon's sitting, just sitting out in the backyard in those cloth-and-wood lawn chairs, and talking about whatever. Times in the woods learning something, anything, instead of visiting everybody every weekend, the people he had to see—his mama, daddy, sisters, cousins. Any talking, his and mine together, happened between visits—on the way from one of them to another—and he acted like he didn't know what to talk about, like most of what he and I might talk about would be wrong somehow, too personal, not the right thing to talk about. About all that was right for Faison and me to hear was what we shouldn't be doing or what we should be doing that we hadn't.

Marilyn and Morgan came with me to the funeral, and June Lee came with Faison.

During the funeral service, Mr. Bass, who used to preach here—he's pretty old now—told about Daddy donating money to the Salvation Army. He told a story about Daddy bringing him some used bricks when he was building a wellhouse. He read the Bible and talked about heaven and the reuniting of loved ones in the glorious hereafter for eternity. He told about Daddy saying he knew he was going to die and that his wife and sisters had taken good care of him in his final years. Glenn Bales, he said, had said he was right with God. Glenn Bales was happy in heaven. Amen. I don't guess Daddy told Mr. Bass that he was right with his sons.

After the service, the pallbearers, Mr. Barham, Mr. Fuller, Mr. Williamson, Mr. Raulings, Mr. Hollingsworth, Mr. Wright, men I have watched grow older and older over the years, rolled Daddy outside and into a black hearse. Faison and I and the others climbed into the family cars and rode in the procession out to the graveyard. Cars meeting us pulled off the road.

At the cemetery I sat in a foldout chair by the grave. After the ceremony, as the family walked to the family cars, Aunt Bette grabbed my coat sleeve and held on.

"When did he *get* here?" she said.

"Sunday morning."

"Why did he come?"

"To visit. He's my uncle, Aunt Bette."

"You going to Miss Laura's funeral tomorrow?" she asked.

"I don't know, I guess so. Why?"

"I was thinking that maybe I could go with you," she said. "I know Ansie is going to stay home. And Faison."

"Well, I don't know right now."

"But listen." She stopped, held on to my sleeve, forcing me to stop. "I ain't going to sit with the family. You can sit with the family, but I ain't. You're welcome to sit with me if you want to. But I ain't going to sit with their family."

"I'll let you know," I said.

Morgan spent that night with me. Uncle Grove was at Faison's. They needed to be apart for a little while. Marilyn insisted on that. She'd caught wind of Uncle Grove's mess, and was all "alarmed" about that. I insisted I could guarantee that Morgan would not die and

178

go to hell in the next two weeks. She knows that for the next two weeks he's mine—and I don't butt in on her time. He played Tetris on his computer most of the late afternoon and night before bedtime. On the way to bed he stopped by the living room where I was unwinding—watching *Fat City*.

"What you watching?" he said.

"*Fat City*." It was the part when Jeff Bridges was trying to keep Stacy Keach from seeing him on the street, right before that ending scene.

"When is Uncle Grove leaving?"

"Sunday."

"I just wish he wasn't such a racist."

"Sit down a minute."

He sat down across from me, sprawled a leg up over the chair arm.

"I want to show you something," I said. I pulled a whittled stick out of my shirt pocket and dropped it onto the coffee table. "There's a story behind that stick. It happened when you were about three, maybe a little younger." And I told him about the time I let him go sailing with a baby-sitter and her cousins, and a storm came up—this was at the coast, in Beaufort. They were supposed to be back at six in the evening. At six-thirty they weren't back, and I'd heard that a boat had capsized in the storm—and that it was a bad storm. I didn't even know if they had life jackets or not. I didn't even know who they were—the baby-sitter's cousins. Marilyn was antiquing and didn't know where Morgan and I were.

While I was sitting there at the dock crazy with worry I picked the stick up off the ground and started whittling. I whittled for half an hour, sitting at the dock in a picnic shelter, waiting in the rain and lightning. I prayed to God that Morgan was alive, safe. I called the Coast Guard. They had no information. While I whittled, I memorized the grain on the stick.

When the boat with Morgan sailed into port, I put the stick in my pocket and saved it. I'd kept it on top of my bookcase all this time.

Morgan sat for a minute after I'd told him all this, then said, "Why did you tell me that?" Typical question.

"I don't know," I said. "It's just a little story. Got me thinking."

"About the stick?"

"Yeah, the stick, and how I've been feeling since my own daddy died. It's been hard. I didn't realize it would make me so tired. And in the middle of that I've been thinking about how I felt that day I thought you were maybe lost in the storm."

"Which was?"

"I was afraid, for one thing."

Morgan reached for and got a peanut from the bowl on the table, popped it into his mouth, and started chewing. "Is that it?" he said.

"Yep. I guess." I was wondering how to get the conversation going again.

"What about the story you told Mother about the medal and all that?"

"Your mother had been in the peace movement. I told her stuff about losing a friend, you know; I told you some about it."

"Why did she say it broke her heart?"

I told him about my daddy not wanting me to go into the war, wanting me to stay home, but I was all for going, all for keeping the world safe for democracy, all for keeping the Vietcong off the shores of California, all that. I called my daddy a coward, as a matter of fact, to his face. I told Morgan about how Uncle Grove had written to Faison and me and said he would go if he could and I wrote him back and said I'd go for all three of us. He sent me a white scarf. And so when I had a choice between Japan, the U.S., and Southeast Asia, I picked Southeast Asia and wrote him and told him so. I was very proud. A fighter pilot going to Vietnam. Too young to have any sense.

That scarf went with me on every mission until the one when my friend got shot down. I was scared, and what I ended up doing was all automatic. It was like I was watching myself go through these automatic mechanical actions. I was in a trance. What I got out of it was a dead buddy and a medal. My old man had been right, in a way. And sometimes, I wish I'd gone to Canada. I'd feel better about some things. Of course that wouldn't have settled with my old man either, but that's what I wish I'd done—sometimes when I think about it all.

After all this, Morgan says, "That's what broke her heart?"

"There was some other stuff. I don't know exactly what it was, but for her I think the story was somehow the basis of a marriage, and looking back, not a really good basis."

"I don't understand," he said.

I told him I wasn't sure I did either.

181

Gloria

Nobody said nothing about me going to either one of the funerals, except Faye, she call me up and invite me to Miss Laura's, so I decided I'd go. In fact, I wore one of Miss Laura's dresses. Faye give me about six, and two of them are very nice, a pink one and a dark blue one. The dark blue one is the one I wore to the funeral, because it was dark.

I been to one other white funeral and I wondered if this one would have any more life to it than the other one did.

It didn't. It didn't have no singing at all. There was just organ music and two preachers said a few words. It didn't seem like one of them knew Miss Laura at all. The other one, Preacher Gordon, came to visit Miss Laura and Mr. Glenn every once in a while. Always spoke to me.

At my church at a funeral of course we get roused up. Because we're in the house of the Lord. The Lord speak to us. Get us moving, after we finish crying. We cry because we feel bad. We sing and shout and praise the Lord because we working up to feel good, and if we don't get to feeling good right after we feel bad then we liable to get stuck feeling bad. These people try to keep from showing anything, so since they don't show they feel bad, they don't have much reason to show they feel good, so you get a quiet service like that one. I can't bring myself to understand it, but they do, and she is one of them so I guess it all works out for the best. They can't just all of a sudden be like they ain't.

Tate and one of his aunts was there. I always get them mix up, but I think this one was Miss Bette. Tate walked over and spoke to me. Fact, several people did. They were real nice. I ask Tate, I say, "What in the world did that *uncle* of yours do?" and he said he got a little disorient. I say, "It sure sound like it." Then he say he and Faison going fishing in a couple of days and take the uncle, his Uncle Grove.

The man—this Grove—dug a grave out in the big white cemetery. Some say he dug it for Mr. Glenn. Some say he dug it for hisself. Sound like he could use a little fishing trip. Bury hisself in the sand like white people do at the beach. I don't understand why they do that.

9

Jimmy

*T*HIS FISHING TRIP.

I didn't know Faison was gone bring his whole family. I knew Tate, his brother, was flying his airplane down to meet us in Beaufort, because he was going to fly on down to Wilmington on the way back home after the trip and pick up four snakes for me. But I thought that was it, just his brother. Their daddy died, see, and this would be a little get-away trip. It ended up that me and Faison drove the truck down with all the fishing equipment and groceries, and flying along with Tate was Tate's boy, the hippy, named Morgan, and this four-hundred-year-old uncle from Arkansas, the one that got in the news when he dug that grave and tried to kill hisself or whatever. Best I could tell he had some kind of breakdown. I was worried about him at first, but then pretty quick after all of us got together it looked like he could take care of hisself. And it looked like the boy was going to keep his mouth shut. He's the one that was on the airplane that time they landed on the back field of that farm, which Faison and Tate, by the way, ended up with one-third of apiece, it looks like. The other third is going to this woman lawyer from Charlotte, their stepsister, I guess it is. Win some, lose some, tie some, and some you just go home. Huh?

So we all met down in Beaufort and drove to Kelly Ford—about forty minutes—crowded in my King Cab. Then once we get there I have to back the truck over this little drop ramp and onto the ferry so our duffel bags, coolers, groceries, beer, fishing gear, and all that can be unloaded onto the ferry for the trip across the sound to the island, McGarren Island. Beautiful stretches of land down there. You just don't know till you see it.

After we unload onto the ferry the old man wants to know why we ain't taking the truck over.

"Nothing but four-wheel drives allowed over," I say.

"Well, why ain't you got four-wheel drive?"

"Well, I don't know. Why ain't you got one?" I'd done found out I could kid around with him. You know. Seemed like he'd seen a lot of action in his time.

"Did anybody bring any hard stuff?" he wants to know.

"Oh yeah. I brought some Jack Daniel's," said Faison. "Just for you. I bought a gallon."

"A gallon?" said Tate.

"We might run into somebody," said Faison.

"We might run *over* somebody," said the old man.

Tate's a tad reserved, you know what I mean. College type. Kept saying he was going bird hunting with us. Never could find the time.

I asked Faison about him once we got rolling. You stand around on the boat, have to talk about something. Faison said he was a psychology teacher. Besides teaching classes, he does experiments, writes about them, stuff like that. "He gets paid, too," he said. "Doing projects for industry companies. Tests for hiring people and stuff like that. Tests to tell if they're crazy. Good money. He's doing a thing on how the deaf and dumb see movies. Strange stuff."

"Drug tests?" I said.

"I don't know if he does that or not. I don't think he does. He actually saw some pretty tough action in Vietnam. He did rescues and recon and directing air strikes. Won a medal. Silver Star or something like that. He got right down there with them and fought it out. Killed a whole bunch of Vietcong. But he won't, you know, talk about it a whole lot." He'd done told me this once.

"It alters a man's life," I said. "At's a fact. It alters a man's life. I saw stuff over there I'll never see again. It's like something settles down on you, makes you different. While we was over there we was different, and I sure as hell don't think anybody ought to get the blame. You can't help what you have to do. You get sent somewhere to do a job, you do the job. I'll tell you one thing," I said. "I by and large loved it. Most of it."

* * *

The ferry holds four vehicles and a load of fishermen. The guys with the four-wheels just leave their stuff in the truck. But since we don't have a four-wheel, we have to pile our stuff on deck and then when we get across in about a hour, Fox will load it—and us—up on his World War II ambulance and take us to our cabin. Fox is this guy works over there for the Captain—Captain Baucom—who leases the land from the government. It's all National Seashore. This little fishing village is something the government lets him do. Fox stays over there all the time because he's wanted for bigamy in three or four states.

The water was rough on the way over. I followed the old man up into the Captain's cabin and sat on this padded bench. The kid wanted to come in, but I closed the door on him and shook my head through the glass. Damn hippy. He follows the old man around.

The old man goes into this story about fishing through holes in the ice. Said he went with a bunch of guys one time and it was so cold that this crazy guy wouldn't pull off his snowsuit to take a crap. It was so cold, and he had to go so bad, he just shit in his snowsuit and figured he'd worry about it later.

Captain eyes us over his shoulder. Ain't nobody else up there but us three.

What happened was, on the snowsuit thing, that night they were all riding back to somewhere in this car and it starts getting hot, and the guy starts unzipping his snowsuit but they don't let him, see. So it gets hotter and hotter and this guy gets to sweating a little and then sweating more and more and the old man is just a-laughing telling all this.

The Captain thinks it's pretty funny, so he starts in and tells six or eight jokes, one after the other, kind of on a roll. Let's see . . . well damn, I can't remember a one. And the Captain is the quiet type. I been over on that ferry quite a few times. He and the old man hit it off.

In a little while, Faison and Tate—and the boy—came on up there and sat for the rest of the trip. I'd step out every once in a while and try to check the wind direction. You ain't gone catch no fish if the wind is from the northeast.

From where we were, the island—less than a mile away—started seeming like it was moving toward us real slow. I always like that part of the trip. I used to come over here six, eight times a year. Lost my first wife that way.

"That wind ain't from the northeast," I said. "It's mostly from the south, southwest." That's the only thing that's important. You ain't gone catch jack shit if the wind is from the northeast. "You ever done any surf fishing?" I asked Tate.

"Nope. Mostly pond fishing."

"I used to fly down here," said the old man, "all up and down this coast before there was much down here. We'd land on the beach and fish out of the surf. Land right on the beach. I don't remember us catching much, but we had a good time landing, usually with a stiff crosswind."

"I just hope we get in the blues," I said. "The big ones. Nothing more fun. Course I ain't gone throw back no trout. You, Faison?"

"No *sah*." Faison turned up his Red, White & Blue. I like old Faison.

I talked to Tate a little while about the snake arrangements—which was for him to meet the snake man in Wilmington at three in the afternoon on Sunday, then fly home with the snakes. The uncle and the boy would be with him.

"You be flying for hire down the line? Anything like that?" I asked him. I sure as hell hoped he wadn't going to come up with a *charge* for this little snake transport. He hadn't said anything about no charges.

"Nothing serious," he said.

"What I need," I said, "is somebody to do a snake run fairly regularly, you know, once, twice a year. Think you might be able to do that? Sort of fit it in with your regular flying?"

"Well, I don't know. Maybe so." He sort of looked at his brother and uncle and I got the feeling he didn't want to be no chicken. Or look that way. You know what I mean.

He asked me what happened to the old snakes, why I had to keep getting new ones.

I told him he'd be surprised how many people will buy them off you when you're doing shows. You talk about snakes in the right way, people will understand they ain't going to necessarily kill you, and they'll be interested in owning one for theirselves, and hell, you can make a little money that way. We talked a little more. You can tell he's a college man. These college people.

I tell you, the stuff I read going on at Duke University. Stuff, people getting eliminated.

189

I don't usually read about the colleges. I, you know, usually hit the front page, the docket, the sports, the funnies. But I was thumbing through and saw this thing about "dead white males." And what it said was there was this group of feminists and abstractionists or some such at Duke University who are trying to cut out everything that dead white males have ever done. I said to myself, Wait a minute! Wait a *minute*!

Think about that. That takes up everything that's ever been done, more or less. Know what I mean? Think about it. These professors are trying to actually destroy all of civilization—or at least the *history* of civilization.

Now, dead white males are actually when you think about it the very ones that's done everything that's ever been done that's important. You got Columbus, you got George Washington, you got, hell, I don't know, George Jones. And these bunch of women and fuzzy-headed asshole men want to just wipe them off the map of history because they're number one dead, number two white, and number three men, the very ones who have killed Indians, fought wars, died in wars, been heroes, while, you know, hell, women were at home having babies and cleaning up baby doo-doo and dusting pianos, and men were, hell, out cutting down trees and stuff like that. It goes against all common sense what they're trying to do.

And all this time the yellow people were all eating with chopsticks and plowing rice with these oxes, and the black people—I'm talking over history—were all whooping it up around some campfire in Africa, and you know, the white males were bringing the world up to where it is today.

190

Now tell me one thing: why don't the colleges work on something like the hunger of little children instead of killing off dead white males?

If they kill off the dead white men, where is that going to leave the live ones—with, I mean, you know, what kind of power base? Answer me that.

I wrote Jesse Helms a letter. And I guarantee you he'll answer it. That is one politician that will give you the time of day. I've wrote him before.

And I don't mean that the problem is, you know, the colleges theirselves. It's the people in them. If somebody would drop the big one in the middle of every kind of college except the agriculture ones, we'd be one hell of a lot better off as far as I'm concerned. Because in the colleges is where things get written down. And I want my race and I want my sex to have some kind of record in the history books of tomorrow. You know what I mean?

"I'll tell you one thing," I said to Tate. "There is some people would kill off dead white men, then go out and feed a sea turtle—some people had rather do *that* than feed a hungry child. You look at some of these research projects put up by the government and the colleges."

He looked at me like I was crazy. So I had to fill him in.

The ferry was slowing down. The dock was a few hundred yards away. It's kind of like a religious experience—coming in over there. Having that dock and everything move toward you real slow. I imagine Columbus and them guys had it all the time, coming up on islands and stuff. The wind wadn't so strong anymore—blocked by the island.

The ferry crew, some high-school student, maybe a college student, I can't tell no more, threw a line to Fox. Fox lives on the island, like I say, because of his legal troubles. He's always tan, and he's got this yellow-white beard. He wears this little camouflage canvas rain hat. He passed the line around a pole and looped it on a bollard. Captain maneuvered the ferry with the engine in forward, *rum-rum-rum-rum*, reverse, *rum-rum-rum-rum-rum*, forward, reverse until it backed up against the loading dock. Fox fastened her to, and then lowered this ramp onto the stern of the ferry, chains rattling and squeaking and all. It's all got in my blood, somehow. "Crank em up," he said. "Four-wheel drive."

The first truck, this red GMC, in reverse, bounced its rear wheels up onto the ramp, then fell back to where it was before. The engine raced and it got up on the ramp—rear wheels, then front wheels. The driver, with his arm up on the seat, looked back through his rear window. Listen. This is funny, now. We were all standing there watching. In other words he wadn't doing a real good job of getting his truck off the ferry. Then all of a sudden this second guy in there, in the truck on the passenger side, this guy that we hadn't seen, sits up. I guess he's been passed out in there or something. He had definitely had a few. Some people come over here to drink instead of fish. Well this guy sticks his head out through the window—his hair was gray and sprayed out in all directions. His eyes were red and brown and wild looking. He started to say something, pulled his head back in partway about time the truck bounced down off the ramp, knocking his head—*bam*—up against the window. Well, the truck turns around and starts off toward the cabins. The passenger door opens. Red brake lights come on. The driver grabs for his passenger, see, but misses. So the man is standing out on the sand, unsteady, looking at the ferry, wild-like, then looking at the ground, around at the cabins off behind him, then back toward the ferry. He staggers, you know, brings his hands to the top of his head and screams, "Where the goddamn hell am I?"

I'll tell you they get all kinds over there.

When all the trucks were off the ferry, Fox backed that old World War II ambulance or utility vehicle or whatever it is onto the ferry, helped us load up our gear, then drove off the ferry and along a sand path toward our cabin. Faison, the old man, and me sat up front with the driver. Tate and the boy sat on the tailgate. I got a strong whiff of the ocean air—bringing that funny feeling to my chest. I looked at the cabins while we headed toward ours, number 14. They all look like old smokehouses and feed shacks.

Fox helped us unload. It didn't take but a minute.

I put up groceries while the others unpacked.

In the cabin was chairs, a table, a two-eyed gas stove, a sink, two sets of bunk beds, and a rollaway. Good thing we had the rollaway. Hell, I tell you, I won't expecting no family reunion.

I scratched my crotch. "Damn, I caught something," I said. "If I got the crabs we can fish with *them*."

"I don't want the bunk under you then," said Faison. "Where you sleeping?"

"I'm on top right there."

"Hell, I'm getting over here, then. Tate, you'll have to sleep under there."

Far as I was concerned the boy would have to sleep in the rollaway. "Hell, I'm just kidding," I said. "I ain't got no crabs." I scratched again. "I got something though."

Faison was ready to hit the beach and I was, too, so that's what we did. Tate and the old man and the boy stayed behind to finish unpacking or something.

Morgan

This place was awesome. It was like something you see on TV. There was nothing but sand and these little shacks and the ocean. That's it. That's all there was. Uncle Faison and Jimmy went on down to the beach to fish. The beach was just beyond these sand dunes that are out behind the back door. They barely took time to unpack. They had all this paraphernalia they were taking with them. The surf-casting rods are *ten to thirteen feet long*. Mine, the one I'm using, is ten feet long. Uncle Faison showed me some stuff about it coming over on the ferry. Uncle Grove said he didn't want to fish.

When Dad, Uncle Grove, and I got to the beach,

Uncle Faison was standing in the surf, knee-deep, fishing. All together in a little camp on the sand were these like lawn chairs, tackle boxes, a cooler, buckets, and a bait fish cut into chunks on a wooden board. We bought the bait fish, about fifteen of them—millet or mullet or something—in Beaufort before we drove to Kelly Ford. Jimmy's got a King Cab and I had to sit in my dad's *lap* between Beaufort and the ferry. We'll be flying to Wilmington to pick up some snakes on the way back. Teresa Charles, this girl I been talking to, made me promise to call her when we get back to let her know how it goes. She thinks it's pretty wild. I didn't tell Mom about the snake part of the trip.

Jimmy, when we got down to the beach, was standing with his rod leaning against his shoulder. What was neat was, he held a small whetstone in one hand and a fishhook in the other. Just under his nose he was sharpening the hook. What was funny was the way he was looking at it cross-eyed, sharpening, looking at it, sharpening. He's got like some kind of strange energy, which being cross-eyed made even stranger.

Uncle Grove says to Jimmy, "Most people won't sharpen hooks." Then he tells him he's sharpened every hook he ever used and they talk about that for a few minutes, and then Jimmy hits him with this question: "Were you really trying to throw in the towel, do yourself in—you know—with the grave and all?" Uncle Grove sort of looks at him like what are you talking about, and then he said something like, "I was. Then I got to thinking about this fishing trip. You can't fish when you're dead. Besides that, it's a sin to kill yourself."

Jimmy goes in to talking about if there is and if there isn't a God, and Uncle Grove tells him if he doesn't believe in God he's going to hell.

All I had to do was put some bait on my hook and like cast. I was using a pair of Jimmy's waders. The water's still too cold from winter to wear just a bathing suit.

Uncle Faison hadn't showed Dad anything about his reel like he had me, and as far as I know Dad hadn't ever been fishing—since they were little anyway. So down on the beach there, Uncle Faison starts showing Dad some stuff about the rod and reel and all.

Dad watched, then kind of grabbed the reel.

"No," said Uncle Faison. "Let me—"

"I got it," said Dad. "I *got* it."

"Okay, okay. Some of this ain't so simple though. At least let me show you how to get the bait on there so it'll hold."

"I can do it. I been fishing."

Dad didn't want anybody to show him anything.

Uncle Grove sat in a chair and didn't fish. I sat beside him and held my rod and reel. Dad, Uncle Faison, and Jimmy had their rods stuck in these rod holders that were stuck in the sand. We were kind of spread around on the beach. They said I could put my rod in a holder, but I wanted my hands on mine.

Uncle Grove said he just wanted to look at the ocean. He was wearing a sweater with holes in it, and he'd stopped shaving, so he looked kind of ratty, and his eyes were bloodshot. He started talking, talking about his "hot head." He said his papa had one, said his papa and some guy named Saul Proffitt would get into a fight over a cow or something like that and his papa—who would be my great-grandad—would jump at Saul with a pitchfork or whatever he could get his hands on. He had a pitchfork at Saul Proffitt's throat one time, he said, and gave it a little jerk-stab like he was going to stab Saul—Uncle Grove is sitting there on the beach kind of acting all this out—and Saul jerked his head back real quick like and hit a nail, nail sticking out of a post. Once Uncle Grove starts talking it's impossible not to listen because of the way he talks and tells.

He went on to tell me that after his daddy died, his mama never said a word to any of the children about marrying this Mr. Harper and that when word came that Mr. Harper had whipped his sister Evelyn, my grandma, that's when he went after him. He was boiling, he said—Uncle Grove—when he stepped up onto the step there at the house and old man Harper was inside. Uncle Grove had moved out by then, and he like told Mr. Harper to come on outside. He could see him in there behind the screen. It was dark in there and him sitting, and he wouldn't even get up. Just sat there. These are the kinds of things that Uncle Grove puts in his stories. Looking through the screen and all like that, so that it seems real. He's got all this stuff from way back in the past pulled up close, real close.

So Uncle Grove went in after him, through the screen door, and they had this pushing-shoving-hitting thing around the living room. After that he said he didn't have anywhere to go but to town, and then he said he got in with the wrong crowd and all. And then there were what he called woman troubles, and some kind of car business, and hauling liquor, and the concessions, and this and that and the other.

All the stuff from last week about the graves was in the newspapers. Aunt Bette and Aunt Ansie blew up I guess when they found out about Uncle Grove being back in town and all. I can't figure out what they've got against him. They cornered me at the funeral home and said that Uncle Grove had been a bad influence on everybody he knew, including his sister, my grandmother. I don't know why they're so obsessed with all that. It happened over forty years ago, her running away. It's like when she left, that was the end of the world.

Mom says she's glad she's out of the family for good.

The sun was getting low in the sky. Uncle Grove had gone back to the cabin. The wind had died down. It was very peaceful. I hadn't been all that sure I'd like it, but it was so peaceful, and *big* out there—so much space and nobody, nothing, way, way down the beach anywhere. The times I've been to the ocean before there were always all these people around and everybody worrying about suntan lotion and all that. But this was different. We'd all sit quiet for a long time and look at the waves rolling and foaming. Uncle Faison and Jimmy would go to the cooler for a beer every once in a while. I'd go for an apple or a Snickers. It was like nobody was going to tell me what to eat or drink. I thought about drinking a beer, but Dad would get all bent out of shape.

There was nothing out there but the ocean and sand and us, fishing. But mainly we were just sitting around. The rods were lined up along the beach in the rod holders, except for mine. I was still holding it. No bites. No nibbles. The sun was hot and the air was cool.

Your mind gets to wondering about things, like it begins to get a little disconnected from . . . from whatever. I would look at the sand and think about counting the grains and I thought about like how long the ocean had been there doing the same thing over and over. I thought about Uncle Grove. I thought about what if my grandma hadn't left—how it would have been different for my dad. I thought about Junior getting killed in the car wreck. There was supposed to be some argument between Uncle Faison and Aunt June Lee that led to the wreck. I've never heard anybody talk about it, but I got that from somewhere.

Jimmy stopped by my chair on the way to the cooler. "One of the best things about this," he said, "is that there ain't no streets and cars over here. You ever think about how much noise cars make?" He was like actually talking to me. "You ever think about back before cars, when everywhere sounded just like iss? You ever think—HOLY SHIT!" he screamed. He pointed.

The rod on the far end of the line was just booking. Dad and Uncle Faison started getting up, which isn't easy in these waders we had to wear. We were sort of scattered around on the beach, far apart. Jimmy was screaming, "YOU GOT A TIT, BATE—A TIGHT, BATE—A BITE, TATE. GODDAMMIT. GODDAMN, THEY'RE GONNA START HITTING. I KNEW IT. I KNEW IT!" He was like going crazy.

It was Dad's rod. He pulled it up out of the rod holder, looked at the reel like he was trying to remember how to hold it.

Uncle Faison grabbed at it, trying to turn the reel handle over some other way or something.

Dad pulled away, keeping the reel in front of him. The end of the rod like suddenly dipped down hard.

"Whoa!" said Jimmy.

The rod suddenly bent even more, dipped, and the reel whined.

"WHOA, LOOK AT THAT!" said Jimmy. "That fish weighs twenty pounds if he weighs a ounce. God," he said, "I hope it ain't no sand shark. Yippee, this is the year. This *is* the year. WHOA, HEY, LOOK, *I* GOT ONE!" He started toward his rod, which was dipping and pumping. "This is the year," he yelled. "This is the year!"

And that's when the first one hit my line. It was like a fist hitting me in the shoulder. It was unreal.

Jimmy

We lined all the fish up on the cleaning table outside the back door—just a-shining. One flapping here, one flapping there. We were about to clean them, all but the boy. He was still on the beach fishing. When they had started hitting, he about flipped, screaming and I don't know what all. His voice is changing and all that.

We went to work on the fish with pliers and fillet

knives. Tate fell behind. I was using my Leatherman tool. Best tool I ever had, except my fingers. Man I used to work for at the sawmill was always saying, "There's no tool like the fingers." Huh?

We skinned, filleted, stopped, drank beer, flipped the fish over, done the same thing on the other side, cut the fillets into steaks, dropped them onto ice in the cooler, drank some more beer. We had twenty-two big blue-fish. Averaging out at twelve to fifteen pound. A real sight.

"Here, let me help," says the old man.

"You're the overseer," said Faison. "You give the orders."

The old man looked like he felt pretty good. He'd had a few.

Tate was standing at the fish-cleaning table, talking to him. "There, Uncle Grove," he said. "Over there. Get that chair and sit down." He pointed to a old stool by the faucet. The old man started over and Tate said to Faison, "He's swaying."

Faison says, "Yeah, I know. Pass me a beer, Jimmy."

"We should have bled them," I said. But hell I didn't have time. You need to cut a bluefish's throat soon as you catch it. Especially the big ones. Just like a deer or a pig.

"Wha's a matter?" said the old man from his chair. "One of 'em ain't dead? Here, I'll shoot his ass." He stood up, reached into his back pocket, pulled out a snub-nosed .38.

"Well, that's a load off my mind," I said.

"Whoa," said Faison, walking over to him. "Here, let me have that."

201

He put the gun back in his pocket and sat down. "Never mind. They're just fish," he said.

Old man made me a little nervous. Not too nervous. But a little nervous.

"That's right," said Faison. "Don't you want to give me that gun?"

"Oh no."

"What the hell you need it for?" asked Tate.

"You never know. You never know."

"Did you know he had that gun?" Faison asked Tate.

"No. Think we ought to take it?"

"Go ahead, if you think you can."

"He ain't going to hurt nothing," I said. "We should've had him shooting down at the beach. That second or third one—second one I hooked—was like he was pulling me out, man. I had to keep, you know, walking out farther and farther. I tell you one thing: for his size, that was the fightingest fish I *ever* caught."

Fox drove up in his truck, got out and walked over. "Looks like you boys had some luck. How do you do, sir?" he said to the old man.

The old man says, "I catch them. They clean them."

"Pretty, ain't they," said Faison.

"They sure are," said Fox. He thumped his cigarette out into the sea oats. "Y'all need anything from the mainland?"

"We might be needing some beer before too long," I said.

"I need a woman," says the old man. "Anna Phillips."

* * *

Later on that night we're eating supper in the cabin. The boy finally come in. He'd caught four more blues, but they were small. I got him out on the cleaning table and showed him how to clean them.

For supper we had fresh, fried bluefish, corn bread, cheese nachos, pork and beans, and beer.

We're sitting around the table after supper, more or less shooting the shit, talking a little about what that farm would bring. So I told them about Timmy winning twelve hundred dollars in a crap game last year. We were feeling pretty good. The man won twelve hundred dollars. This really happened. As soon as he won the money he decided we'd go live in a condominium on a golf course for a week. Wherever that is—Pinehurse. I tell all about the trip—crazy trip—and then the old man, he's feeling pretty good by now, starts in.

"Hell, I been to Pinehurse," he says, "right when they come out with electric golf carts. I was down there with Merle Mayberry, a guy I was in business with. I never played no golf, but he had two sets of clubs, see. And he let me play with the god-awful one. We get down there and we rent two carts. Him and the other fellow got one, and I got the other one. Hell, I ain't never been on no *golf* cart. Merle has. I ain't. He tells me to follow them on over to the place where you practice hitting it."

The old man is going good. He can tell a story, and we're just sitting there listening, with all the time in the world. There's nothing else to do on the island.

"Well, hell," he says, "I didn't know them golf carts don't make no noise. So I figure it won't crank, so I get mad and stomp on the gas pedal and wham, I run into this sweet gum tree and shake all the golf clubs out the back and roll back over 'em and so forth and so on. Crazy.''

The boy cracks up. It was pretty funny.

''And let me tell you, them clubs really won't worth two cents. Well, I finally get to hitting them pretty good over at the hitting place, and I let go this swing, hit the ball, dribble it off to the side, and the club you know I'm holding up over my head feels real light somehow, and so I look up and there goes the damn club head, sailing through the damn air.''

I was cracking up, too, sipping on a cool one, smoking a cigar, leaning back in my chair, listening to the ocean crash a couple hundred yards away. The life.

''Well, hell,'' the old man says, ''now I'm standing there with this *pool cue* in my hands, right? In front of, you know, forty, fi'ty millionaires.'' He'd pulled his chair out from the table, kind of out into the center of the room.

''Well, I look out across the field and here comes the . . . this guy in the little caged-in green tractor. *He's bringing me the damn club head back*—in front of everybody, in front of these forty, fi'ty millionaires. So I took it, put it in my front pocket, and that looks pretty odd, and Merle is about to die laughing.''

''Then I lose the head to my other wood—same way, fourth or fifth hole—and that bag of clubs looks pitiful. No wood things, just a bag of sticks. I played maybe two, three times since then. You boys ever play any golf?''

''I played a couple of times,'' said Faison. ''I ain't no good, though. I played with my mama one time.''

Things got quiet.

"When did y'all play golf?" said Tate. He seemed a little shook. He still hadn't drunk no beer or nothing.

"She took me to the Putt-Putt over across from the Taylors' house. That Putt-Putt they had on Highway Twelve. You remember that Putt-Putt, don't you? Probably one of the first there ever was. Had that great big WHITES ONLY sign across the front."

"I remember that place," I said. I did.

Tate says he never knew his mama took Faison to the Putt-Putt. A little family stuff, here.

"Evelyn was something," said the old man. "She could plow, do anything I could, growing up. Plowed that little old crooked-legged mule like a man."

"She die?" I asked. I didn't know nothing about this stuff. How was I supposed to know what was coming?

"She left home," said Faison, "when I was seven and Tate was about six months old."

So I said something about being glad me and Timmy had a good mama and Faison says, "I don't think she was necessarily bad. She just got tired of farm life, I think. Hell, I did too."

"She was a good woman," said the old man. "It was all kind of sad. She left. Then five years later, I left."

"So she was your sister?" I asked the old man.

"Right. She was a good one, too."

"Do you know why she left?" the boy asked the old man.

It was quiet again, almost like somebody else had just walked in the room. Spooky. I could tell that it was one of those things in families that nobody talks about. Like Timmy's stuff.

"Yeah, I do know, but it's well enough left alone. I took care of it more or less," says the old man.

"Did she just leave?" said the boy. Pressing, see.

"Leave it alone," said Faison. "What's the big deal? She left, she left."

"I guess it's a big deal to me," said Tate to the old man, "if you know something we don't." Tate was sort of leaning forward, serious-like, his elbows on his knees, looking the old man in the eye.

"She left," said the old man—and he looked right at Morgan—"she left because she was funny, you know, queer, she left so she could kissy-kissy with another woman, some dyke with a English accent. That's what happened."

I'm thinking, hold on, this is *too* serious.

Faison kind of laughed. "You're lying."

"So help me God that was it," says the old man.

Faison stood up like he was going somewhere, took a couple of steps, turned around, then sat back down. "She ran away with a *woman*?" he says.

"That's right." The old man was wetting down a cigar.

"Bullshit. I knew her. She might have been unhappy or something, but she won't no queer." Faison looked like he might be a little mad at his uncle.

"You're right. You're right. I don't think she was either," said the old man. "That's the whole problem. What happened was this woman from England talked her into it. She was a smooth-talking dyke that come from England, through New York, and took advantage of her. That's what it was."

So they get to going back and forth, you know, about

all this stuff that happened, hell, something like forty, forty-five years ago and the old man tells them they ain't got nothing to worry about, that he took care of every-thing—that he paid them a visit and roughed up the one from England enough that she and their mama, they split up for good. I about cold-cocked the kid because he wants to know what's wrong with being a lesbian. Butts in, asking that shit. I about cold-cocked him.

So here I am fishing on McGarren Island with some sixteen-year-old weirdo, sitting around the supper table drinking beer, and suddenly all this strange stuff comes out, and Mr. Weirdo wants to know what's wrong with lesbians. You figure it. So I told him. Anybody with any sense knows you behave the way you want other people to behave—if you've got any ethics to you. That's the bottom of the Christian tradition which is the foun-dation of America and so you got these homosexuals behaving in such a way that if *everybody* did, then the human race would *peter out* so to speak. In other words, we're talking the elimination of the whole human race, and here's a sixteen-year-old so-called leader of tomor-row wanting to know what's wrong with *that*. You fig-ure it. I didn't want to waste the breath to try to explain it. His old man didn't even look at him. He just sat there looking at the wall like he hadn't ever *seen* a wall.

Honour

I knew about Evelyn's brother. Evelyn had talked about him often. But I couldn't have imagined the extent of his . . . his brutality.

The people I've always lived around have been tolerant—in the main. This man was bloody evil. He'd been arrested for something over near the mines and she'd been to visit him in jail and I guess gave him our address, because he came. She had gone into town that afternoon. But he came right on in the house anyway, like he owned it. He sat down on the settee and said, "So you're the queer."

"Pardon?" I said.

He stood up and screamed at me, language I will not repeat, and had wrestled me to the couch—his pants unbuttoned, and down—when Evelyn came in. Thank god she came in. Furniture was upset and a lamp was broken. It's with me to this day. And the horror of it all—really the main horror of it all, if you want to know the truth—was that Evelyn, even after that, *would not chastise him*. She talked to him until he promised he would leave and not come back. And then she hugged him before he left. She hugged him. I was sitting there, shaking, crying, red welts on my arms, deaf in one ear, and she hugged him good-bye.

After that, Evelyn was not Evelyn, and I was not Honour. There was no bridge back. I packed and said good-bye to Evelyn and my house. There was no choice and I knew I could never return. I've left many places, but this leaving was the most difficult. And I haven't seen her since. My Evelyn. I often wonder how she is, where she is, what she may be doing. We memorized so much about each other.

Jimmy

Late that night I stood out in the surf fishing, watching that sparkling stuff, phosphorus or whatever, around my waders, then looking out to the ocean, feeling the pull of that four-ounce weight on the bottom, waiting for a big fish to knock the hell out of it so I could get all that fighting going, dragging and pumping that rascal in.

The old man had gone to bed—he was washed out—but Weirdo and Faison and Tate were fishing. Lights scare the fish so we were in the dark. We had a little penlight at the bait board. More stars out there than I've ever seen anywhere. It's always like that down there.

Finally the boy went in. He'd already been so tired he couldn't hardly walk. He probably can't help the way he is. Faison said he has a weird mama. And he gets all that lesbian stuff from the public schools.

The going stayed slow, so I finally walked in the surf over to Tate. I was mellowed out a little bit, I suppose. I figured he was getting that way, too. He'd finally started drinking, filled him a flask before we came out after supper. But he hadn't said much.

We stood there together holding our rods and reels.

"Hey," I said, "if we don't catch another fish it's all been worth it. There are a lot of people in the world don't like to fish," I said, "but I'll tell you one thing, a night like this, a surf rod in your hands, a cooler of beer on the beach, a mess of fried bluefish in your belly, it's the life. Second best thing to pussy."

He didn't say nothing.

"Yep," I said.

"That's right," he said. Took a couple of steps away from me. Something having to do with psychology and all that. He tried to say at supper that if his mother *was* queer, it didn't make no difference to him. Yeah. Sure thing. You could tell he didn't mean it.

"Nothing better," I said. "You know of anything better?" Seeing if I could loose him up a little.

"I'd say this ranks right up there," he said.

"Yep. Didn't Faison say you flew fighters in Vietnam?"

"That's right."

"That must have been kind of like flying a machine gun."

"Never thought about it that way, but yeah, that's right. Kinda that way."

"I had a cousin had six machine guns."

"That's a bunch."

We fished without saying anything for a while.

"I'm glad you can go get the snakes for me," I said.

"Oh. Yeah."

After another few minutes, he reeled in, walked up

to our little beach camp. Faison reeled in, walked over. Then Faison said they were turning in. I said I was going to fish till two and if I hadn't had no bites, quit then.

Faison

Me and Tate get back and sit on the porch so we won't wake Uncle Grove and Morgan. The cabin had a little porch and a couple of lawn chairs. Tate pulled off his waders, then his socks, and shook them out. You could see in the starlight.

I told him his feet stinked.

"Maybe they really smell sweet," he says. "Think about it."

I told him he was crazy.

"No, no, no. Think about it," he says. "You know the whole existence, the very whole existence exists in our minds and in our minds only. I been thinking about this." He draped his socks over the railing.

I said, "You hear Uncle Grove's snowsuit story?"

Didn't faze him. "Wait a minute," he says. "Listen. I mean all beliefs about everything are in our heads, not out there in the world. Tha's where everything is and always will be unless we take our brains out our heads, so that means that what somebody *believes* is their whole world. See?''

"No, I don't. What is this? Philos'phy? Psycho'gy?'' Tate gets off on this crap sometimes. But I hadn't seen him this looped in fifteen years. "The difference between me and you, Tate,'' I said, "is I *know* stuff, and you know *about* stuff. Hit on that, you want to talk some philos'phy. Hit on that.''

"Shit, Faison. You damn redneck,'' he says.

I had one of my socks halfway off. "You drunk, Tate. I know what it is. Are you talking all this crap because you think it means Mama should get off the hook for being queer? Is that it?''

"I hadn't said that. I'm talking something different. Try to think for a change. And listen very carefully to what I'm about to say. And *think* about it. The way something smells is not in this world. It's in our heads, because if it was in the world then you wouldn't have flies landing on shit, because shit would stink to flies, too, to everybody, to all living creatures. Why you think a goddamn fly will land on shit instead of a flower? Because a turd smells good to them, that's why. In his head, it's beauty and in ours it's ugly . . . ugliness. Who's to say? Who's to say? That's what I say. Who's to say? And think about this: We see light waves. What if we saw sound waves? We been conditioned by the kind of waves we see. Think about—''

"I don't have to listen to all this, Tate,'' I said. He was looped. "You talk like a damned atheist. I need a beer.'' Then I told him, "You won't ever get over going to college, Tate, you know that?'' I got up, opened the beer cooler, got out a beer. When I had raised the lid

212

to the cooler I had this sudden understanding—this golden thought more or less. So I said, "If the world is in your head, then why can't you catch a fish in your head? Why you got to come to the damn ocean? Answer me that one."

Jimmy came up. "Catch a fish in your head?" he says. "Whoa."

"We just talking some bullshit," I said. "Philos'phy."

"That's a load off my mind," he says. "Count me out." He stepped over to the beer cooler. "Who needs a beer?"

"Not me," said Tate. "You do any good?"

"Naw."

"I'll take one more," I said. "No, wait a min. I awawready got one right here. Hell, I'm be up all night pissing."

"I'll piss for you," said Jimmy.

Tate laughs, lights up a cigar. And he don't smoke, either. The glow was bright in the dark.

"What a day," said Jimmy. "What a day. Best hour of fishing I ever had in my life. I tell you one thing," he said, lighting him a cigar, too. He shook out the match. "I tell you one thing." He blew out a puff of smoke. He pushed a flip-top box of cigars toward me. "Here, have one," he said. I took one. He drew on his, looking at it, his eyes kind of crossed. "I tell you one thing . . ."

"Wha's that?" I said.

He looked at me, thought for a few seconds. "I forgot," he says. "Wait a minute, I know what it was. Die ever tell you bout the tie we stayed in a condo?"

"You told us at supper," I said.

"That's right. I thought I did. Whoa. Who far'ed?"

"Don't say fart," I said, "we get a speech from Tate bout how a fly goes to college."

"Eat shit, Faison."

"I've *always* been able to whip your ass, Tate. I can do it right here, now, too." I would, too. In a minute.

But all the time I was talking, I was thinking: Mama was a lesbian. Uncle Grove didn't have no reason to make up something like that. If I hadn't known her it would be different. That's why it don't make no difference to Tate. He didn't know her. I had actually known the woman. The first and last lesbian I ever knew, I guess. That's a hell of a thing.

Jimmy went in in a minute and Tate was laying on the porch on his back, getting sauced, more sauced. He talked some out of his head and I just kind of went along with him. Then he asked me this—and I could tell from his tone of voice that he'd all of a sudden got real, real mad—he asked me did I know I didn't say good-bye when I left home thirty, thirty-five years ago. Hell of a thing. I didn't remember anything about that. I was a kid. Then he asked me if I'd say I was sorry. He was raised up off his back and staring at me. I said, "Sure. I'm sorry I didn't say good-bye." Hell, I didn't remember anything about that.

Then we were talking about Junior's footstone and he agreed with me about the name. I was kind of surprised that he actually went right along with my line of thinking about all that.

"You and June Lee made an agreement, didn't you?" he said.

"Right. A promise."

"Well, I think that ought to stand. I mean it's not like you and him didn't get along. Y'all got along great. And him and his first daddy didn't get along at all, and so it makes perfect sense that he'd be named after you. What's on that footstone will be around one hell of a lot longer than you, or me, or June Lee, and let's face it, this guy was a asshole. And for sure y'all would have adopted him. It ought to be Faison Bales, Junior, on there. I'm with you one hundred percent, Faison. You know, Junior was like Uncle Grove, too, you know what I mean? I mean you know what I mean? Even though he won't blood kin."

I swear it was hard to talk about Junior out there under that sky, knowing how much he would have loved to be there. "That's right. And you know, we're talking about passing something along. You got Morgan. You're passing something along." And then I wondered if he'd been expecting *me* to pass something along to *him* back when I was a kid.

And I'm thinking, what if you can't pass nothing along? See what I mean? About Junior. And see, I knew Junior was this other guy's son. I mean by blood, right? But I figured by the time I got him going fishing and hunting with me enough, a good bit of me would wear off on him. Enough for a name change, at least. It'd be like he really was my son. And June Lee agreed right down the line. And then in the end she got pissed off cause I hadn't ever told her I was married before. I mean, that didn't have nothing to do with it, for Christ's sake.

"You know what I wish sometimes?" says Tate. "I mean, deep down?"

"Wha's at?"

"I mean don't tell nobody this."

"I won't."

"Sometimes I deep down wish that Morgan was a little more like Junior was. He ain't ever been that way at all."

"Hell, who knows, just be glad Morgan ain't dead, Tate, that's all I got to say. That's all I got to say. Just be glad."

We didn't talk no more, and when we went to bed finally it was getting the slightest bit light in the east. Just the slightest bit. I reckoned Mama might already be dead and why the hell should I worry about something happened over forty years ago. It's all history. I can't do a thing about it. I can't do nothing about Junior either, but be sure his name stays what it is on that footstone.

10

Morgan

I FINALLY TOLD TERESA THE WHOLE STORY ABOUT
the cut on my forehead. We were at the lake, parked,
talking before we, you know. I held off until then. It
was in me like an explosion waiting to get out. The
story. It had just happened and nobody hardly knew
yet. So I told her.

What happened was—and this really happened—after
the fishing trip, Dad, Uncle Grove, and I took off from
Beaufort and flew to Wilmington to pick up these four
snakes. What we were supposed to do was fly them on
into Summerlin for this guy Jimmy, who we went fishing with. He does snake shows and stuff like that.

It was my dad flying in the one seat up front and in

the wide backseat was Uncle Grove and me. And behind us on top of the storage compartment was a snake
cage with this small notched stick through the latch
holding the top down, see.

We landed in Wilmington and spotted the snake guy
and followed him over to his truck. He was this little
guy with a mustache and big hands. He shook the four
rattlesnakes from his cage down into our cage. Two big
ones, a medium, and a small. The rattles all started up,
then died down. Awesome.

"They're all feisty," the guy said. "I ain't had them
long." He looked at me. "You ever seen fangs close
up?"

"Nope." I kind of stepped back.

He had this stick with a metal hook on the end. He
stuck it down in the cage, slid it around the small rat-
tlesnake, and pulled it up. All the snakes' rattles started
up again. He dropped the snake on the ground, pinned
the head with the hook, reached down with another stick
that had a rope loop on the end and looped it around the
snake's neck, pulled it tight, and then lifted up the snake.
It wrapped around the stick. He pressed the hook into the
snake's mouth and opened it wide so that these two little
white, you know, like nipple things dangled down. Then
it looked like he pressed harder, and these two white,
sharp, curved bone-needles came pushing out. One was
dripping. Really.

"Piece of work, ain't it?" he said.

Uncle Grove is standing there with his hand on his
back pocket. See, here's the deal. He carries a *pistol*.
You know, he's the same one dug the grave and all that
was in the newspaper.

The man drops the snake back in with the others. All the rattles started up, sounding like bees. It was like spooky. But you ain't heard nothing. Listen to this.

Dad stuck the little stick back through the latch, then paid the guy the ninety dollars or whatever it was this Jimmy guy had given him, and we like took off.

When we were about fifteen miles south of Horseshoe Lake—that's where Dad said it was—the engine suddenly got very loud, like the muffler was out or something. Dad kind of started grabbing at things, then there was this powerful vibration. Then, get this, the engine stopped and the propeller *froze*. Everything was very quiet, except for the wind whistling.

"What's wrong?" says Uncle Grove.

I couldn't say anything. I was too . . . I don't know, stricken or something.

Dad looked back over his shoulder at the snakes. His face was white. Then he said he was going to try to restart the engine. We're in this slow, quiet glide, just gliding along, and he starts doing this stuff to restart it but nothing is happening. That propeller up front is staying still, pointing up to about the one o'clock position.

I felt this block of heat moving from my chest up my neck. Then it was ice. "I don't know what's wrong," says Dad. "Something blew. We'll have to put her down somewhere." Then he goes on his mike, like. "Mayday, Mayday, Mayday. Piper two six six two X-ray. Engine failure." And all this.

An answer comes over the radio. "Roger, Piper, this is Cessna four seven two three Charlie." Something like that.

"Loud and clear, Cessna, but I've lost my engine and I'm landing. Please launch a search and rescue," Dad says. He tells them where he is—gives them some kind of numbers and all that.

"This ought to be interesting," says Uncle Grove.

"We got some pastures up here," says Dad. "It shouldn't be any problem. We'll just land in one. I'm shutting off the fuel and electrical systems." His voice was kind of shaking.

I'd think about the ground down there in front and then I'd think about those snakes in back. I looked and one was in a corner alone and three were stacked on top of each other, very still, like they were sleeping.

"Shouldn't we throw them snakes out?" says Uncle Grove.

"No. Not now," says Dad. "We'll be all right."

Out to the right and below was an old barn but I didn't see a house. The ground was flying under us fast, now that we were close to it. It was quiet. No engine. Just wind whistling. We were like just gliding down quietly. There was a big pasture out in front of us. Then Dad was saying something about bouncing over a barbed-wire fence when we—*bam*—hit, and bounced, but what happened was the main gear caught this barbed wire Dad was trying to bounce over, and held. My head snap-banged forward and back off the front seat, the metal part—that's where I got the cut. The airplane flipped upside down and landed on the top and skidded, tail-first, along the ground. I watched the ground shoot out behind us, right there at my head, going away from us while we traveled along backwards, upside down, across this pasture. I just hung from my seat and watched dirt and grass fly out behind us, wondering when we would stop. All the baggage from the baggage compartment—thermal blankets, ropes, oilcans, maps, life preservers, flashlight, rags—all this stuff was flying and bouncing every which way and I knew I'd been hit hard on the head.

Finally, the airplane slid to a stop. We all hung by our seat belts, *upside down*. I could see out through the front window where we'd been, a kind of path along the grassy ground. And listen, right up there in front, wedged between the dashboard, or instrument place, or whatever it is, and the windshield, was the snake cage— open.

The first sound I heard was this fuel leaking and kind of gurgling in the tanks, and then, all around in the cockpit, this dry-bones buzzing of the rattles. I smelled gas—strong—and this electric-like smoke.

The rattles stopped. We were just hanging there, quiet. I was looking at the midsection of a big snake, moving— the rest of him was covered by a thermal blanket and a life preserver. A yellow streak ran down his back through the designs. Another one's head rose up. Then I realized: it was the *same one*.

"Morgan?" said Dad. "You okay?"

"I'm okay."

"I'll *be* okay," said Uncle Grove, "soon as I shoot these snakes. Shit, I thought you were landing on the damn wheels, son."

"Wait a minute. Wait," said Dad. "Don't shoot nothing yet. Just stay real still. I think—"

"Don't turn around," I said. "There's a snake right there behind your head."

221

KA-BLOOM. The snake's head just exploded, like delete. All the rattles started up like mad.

"Got one," said Uncle Grove.

"Wait a minute," said Dad. "We could—"

"Shouldn't we get out?" I said. There was a burning smell and a gas smell. You understand we were hanging upside down and the snakes were in the ceiling right above, or below, our heads.

The whole time I'm telling the story Teresa is like holding tighter and tighter to my arm and her eyes are getting more and more afraid and the whole feeling in the car there at the lake is getting intense, if you know what I mean. I don't believe in you know putting the move on somebody like being aggressive or anything like that but she was all eyes and ears and hands and squeezing and stuff, so I kept telling her the story but I wanted to kind of hurry up and get to the end, so I guess I rushed it some, but I got in the part where I had to shoot a snake before we got out—Uncle Grove lost his glasses, told me how to aim and everything— and how we all crawled out with Dad screaming at us to get out, and then the plane caught on fire, like WHOOSH, like a big ball of fire with just the tail and wings sticking out of all this black smoke going up into the sky, and finally the last snake came crawling out of the fire, on fire himself, and finally burned up and died wiggling this way and that.

We were sitting on this little rise watching all this. It was something.

Teresa wanted to see the cut on my head, so I pulled back the bandage and showed her. Eleven stitches. The car windows were steamed up by now. We were in our own little world. I don't mean to brag or anything, but I think she's in love with me—it was one of those times that there might as well not be one thing on the outside of that car or anywhere else in the world, because nothing else counts when you're at the lake, in a car, with somebody you really, really like a whole lot. And we didn't, you know, like actually *do* anything. But we came so close that it was like the end of the world.

I'm glad I've got that story, now. The snake story. It'll last me my whole life.

11

June Lee

*F*AISON AND ME WERE SITTING ON MY COUCH. OR
our couch.

Tate done this stupid thing and crashed his airplane.
They got out okay though. And Faison's Uncle Grove—
somebody found out all about him and he's going to be
on "Donahue," somebody said. He broke his ankle in
the crash and two newspapers sent people to talk to him
about all the uproar he's caused in the last week. His
people picked him up yesterday and took him back to
Arkansas.

"Why would Tate go get snakes in a airplane?" I
asked Faison.

"I don't know. Why not?"

"Why not? Faison. Look at what happened and answer your own question."

"Same thing could have happened in a car."

"Oh, no it couldn't have," I said.

"I just wish I'd been there."

"Faison."

Faison put his arm up on the back of the couch, and started in on his mother again. "Do *you* think maybe she could have been a lesbian?" All this came up at the beach.

"I don't know," I said. "I wouldn't know what to believe, except your Uncle Grove is crazy. I'm just glad nobody got hurt bad in the crash."

"Yeah. Oh well. Where are those journal things?"

"In the box on the kitchen table. You want another piece of pie?"

"No."

I got up and went to the kitchen and got Junior's blue spiral-bound notebook and took it in to Faison. "Here." I showed him where to start.

I'm glad I was finally able to look at his school stuff, and when I did, I came across these things his fifth-grade teacher, Mrs. McGhee, got him to write in a notebook.

Junior

September 28, 1988
Things I like to do.

My daddy took me fishing yesterday. The first time
he took me I played with the worms the whole time in
the floor of the boat. I was five years old. That day we
had belony sandwiches and oatmeal cookies and Pepsi
cola. I like to fish a lot. I cought a 7 pound bass one
time and we been deep sea fishing some too. I cought
27 spanish makerels in one day. One morning we got
up at 5:15 in the morning. Man I was sleepy. When we
got there they wouldn't go out becase it was to roufht.
We went to a place and ate breakfast and I got backon
and eggs. We tried to find another boat to go out but
everybody was afraid to go out becase of the storme.
We didn't catch anything yesterday, but sometimes thats
the way it is.

October 3, 1988
Pets.

My mamma has a cat, but my daddy won't let it come
in the house because he says no animal should come in
the house. But he is going to get me a bird dog which
can be my pet and at the same time he will be my
daddy's hunting dog. Then when I get old enough I will
go hunting to. Percy Bledsoe has a german shepard that
follows us everywhere we go.

November 3, 1988
Uncles.

My uncel is uncel Tate. He was a hero in the war.
He was a pilot and he rescued a man that got shot down
in his airplane. I am intended to be a pilot someday. If
I get a chance I will probably be a hero in a war too.
That is one way I would have a lot of girlfriens after
me, but I wouldn't want them. I would like to fight for
America. My daddy would have if he hadn't been too
old. My first daddy did fight in the war but he never
told me anything becase I was to young to know what
he said. My daddy has got a uncel named Uncel Grove.
He lives way over there in Arkansas.

November 18, 1988
Aunts.

I've got two aunts who are "great" aunts and two
aunts in Kentucky. My "great" aunts grew up on a
farm and they know how to cook good.

January 5, 1989
Grandparents.

My grandmother ran off when she was not very old
because she was sad and something was wrong with
her. My daddy was a little boy. My aunts raised my
daddy and uncel Tate. One of them gave me a lawnmower to take apart. I like to take apart things. Daddy
showed me how to keep up with all the parts. He said
it was a secret about how to do it so I'm not going to

tell anybody. It has to do with where to put the parts. I'm looking for a bigger one to take apart. I will be able to have a airplane like Uncel Grove had that I seen pictures of and if I can take it apart then I would be able to fix it if it wouldn't start. Somebody in my family had a floatplane. My daddy has a picture of Uncel Grove and his airplane with some writing on it. My aunt gave me that old lawnmower but it stayed over at her house.

January 9, 1989
Things I like to do.

My daddy took me hunting yesterday. He killed 6 quales. When I am 12 I will get a four ten shotgun. My daddy and mama fight sometimes but my mama makes my daddy keep talking so they can make up. My mama broke some dishes on purpose one time. But they are in love anyway. Sometimes they get mushy and pukey. I will not get married until after America goes to war. I will be a pilat in the Air Force or on a carriar like my uncel Tate who was a hero. When I get the shot gun that was handed down from the slaves I will be grown and will have to share it with my cousin Morgan who is a dufus. Then I will get married.

12

Wilma Fuller

I WAS OVER AT MISS IVY TERRELL'S YESTERDAY, POOR thing. She's finally in bed sick sure enough, and I'm glad she's got Gloria looking after her.

She wanted to know if that boy that won the scholarship to Duke was in the same Bales family that had all those carrying-ons a couple of years ago. She'd met Miss Laura once a long time ago. She didn't know none of the rest.

"Well, see," I said, "June Lee, the one married Faison—which was Miss Laura's stepson—June Lee had been going to see Preacher Gordon when that wreck happened and killed her little boy in, what, eighty-nine? and I thought, and I guess everybody else thought that when that happened, and she had this big fight with Faison about the tombstone, that that was the end of their, you know, marriage. And I never thought they'd get back together after a tragedy like that. Tragedies like that can tear a family apart. I especially didn't think they'd agree on that tombstone, but there it is right out there in the cemetery right now, as big as day, and has been out there some time: 'In Memory of Junior' with the dates. A brand-new tombstone.

"I think it's odd not to have the boy's full name on there, but they both seem happy with it, so of course I'm not going to say anything and, Harold, I hope you won't either. It's a free country I always said. Of course nowadays people don't take any responsibilities, don't feel responsible for nothing except theirselves. Nobody visits anymore.

"Harold, put that pillow up behind Miss Ivy's back. She looks a little uncomfortable . . . There, that's better. Anyway, then all that about them graves, about the time Glenn and Laura died—have you ever in your life heard of such a mess? And I knew ever one of them that was involved as good as I know Harold here, almost, and then that Lord have mercy plane crash. It was all Grove McCord's fault. He was Evelyn's brother. Evelyn was the one that left Glenn way back when. You—did you know about that? . . . I wadn't sure. Nobody knew what happened to her, you know, until Grove finally spilled the beans, and told the boys, her boys, Tate and Faison, all about how she had this fatal disease and decided she couldn't put Glenn and her boys through it, that she could face it only if she was off somewhere by herself. So she went to Washington State where there were these springs called Warm Springs and she finally recovered after several years and started back home, but found out about Glenn marrying Miss Laura, so she settled in Tennessee—in Jackson, Tennessee—and taught school until she died, not that long ago. I was glad to get the truth on it, because there had been rumors. Grove told all this before he finally went on back to Arkansas.

"Well, of course after Mr. and Mrs. Bales died, first it looked like Glenn's boys and Miss Laura's daughter would get the farm because it was only normal with that joint ownership thing, and without a will it would go straight to the children. And of all things, nobody thought to look at the deed. Nobody had give that a thought, and then when they were about to split everything up, there it was. The *deed*. Where Glenn's papa had said in some kind of something clause that if any of his children were alive when Glenn died, then that land would have to be sold straight to the oldest for one dollar, and so on down the line till the last one. It just shocked everybody. Nobody had seen it, tucked away in the deed.

"Well, Glenn had two sisters left, Bette and Ansie. Bette's the oldest, and she managed to shake up a dollar, and they both moved right in—her and Ansie—cause it's bigger and nicer than both those little houses over on Tully Drive where they were living, and now there they are, doing just fine.

"Of course you probably know they've put in for Gloria for when you . . . get to feeling better, Miss Ivy. I'm glad you've got her for now, though. Gloria was so good about everything when Glenn and Evelyn died."

"Laura, not Evelyn," says Harold.

"That's right. I got so I can't remember nothing, Miss Ivy. I guess I had Evelyn on my mind, leaving that baby that was still at her breast like she did. I wish I knew what she had, but I guess some things will have to just remain a mystery. I guess we ought to be thankful for mysteries. But it is hard to believe somebody would leave a baby that was at her very breast.

"You know my little brother, Fred, was so long breast-feeding that my mama finally told him that if he'd just stop, for gracious sakes, she'd let him start smoking.

"Harold, where are you going? Get that little box of . . . get that little pretty we brought Miss Ivy out of the truck. We forgot.

"That Harold is a something. By the way, Miss Ivy, would you be interested in buying a bird?"